Kitty Valentine Dates a Hockey Player

Spin the wheel.
Jillian Dodd

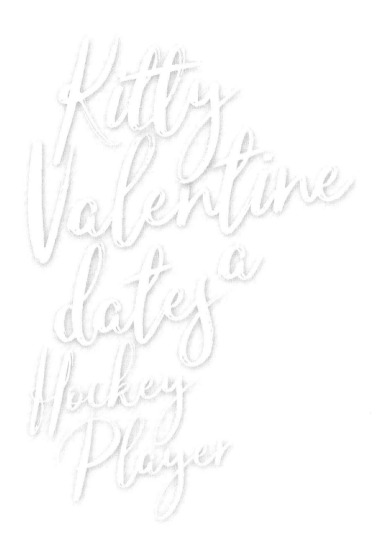

Kitty Valentine dates a Hockey Player

JILLIAN DODD

Jillian Dodd, Inc.
Madeira Beach, FL
Jillian Dodd is a registered trademark of Jillian Dodd, Inc.

Editor: Jovana Shirley, Unforeseen Editing,
www.unforeseenediting.com

ISBN: 978-1-953071-46-0

Books by Jillian Dodd

London Prep

London Prep: Book One
London Prep: Book Two
London Prep: Book Three

The Keatyn Chronicles

Stalk Me
Kiss Me
Date Me
Love Me
Adore Me
Hate Me
Get Me
Fame
Power
Money
Sex
Love
Keatyn Unscripted
Aiden

Kitty Valentine Series

Kitty Valentine dates a Billionaire
Kitty Valentine dates a Doctor
Kitty Valentine dates a Rockstar
Kitty Valentine dates a Fireman
Kitty Valentine dates an Actor
Kitty Valentine dates a Best Man
Kitty Valentine dates a Cowboy
Kitty Valentine dates a Hockey Player

That Boy Series

That Boy
That Wedding
That Baby
That Love
That Ring
That Summer

Spy Girl Series

The Prince
The Eagle
The Society
The Valiant
The Dauntless
The Phoenix
The Echelon

Love Series

Vegas Love
Broken Love
Fake Love

Girl off the Grid

compelling." I have to snicker as I raise what's left of my drink. "Apparently, I'm not exciting or compelling when I'm writing strictly from my imagination. I guess all the people who read my first few books didn't know what they were talking about when they posted such glowing reviews."

"That doesn't sound like Maggie. Didn't you tell me she asked if she was pushing too hard at one point?"

"Yeah, well, I guess now that she's given me six months off, she's not so concerned anymore."

The fact is, Maggie's patience is waning. Every single tick of the clock reminds me that I'm wasting time, that my publisher expects certain things from me in return.

"So, I guess it's time for this, huh?" Hayley reaches into her bag, fishing for the spinner, and places it on the table.

I've come to both love and hate the spinning wheel she put together for me when this whole crazy experiment started.

But it's for my career, and she's right. I've worked too hard to let things fall apart just because I have a crush on someone. The more I think about it that way, the easier it is for me to adjust to the idea of finding somebody new to date.

Even if I'd rather be dating the infuriating, fascinating, annoying, sexy-as-sin, and sweet-when-he-feels-like-it guy across the hall.

I rub my hands together. "Okay, let's see who

the lucky guy will be this time." Wow, that almost sounds hopeful and positive. If things ever do go permanently south in my writing career, maybe I could take up acting instead.

When my next trope appears, we shoot each other a skeptical look.

"Hockey?"

She shrugs. "Well, sports romance is a big deal. Even I know that, and your books are the only fiction I read."

"But hockey? That's, like, the one sport I know the least about. It takes place on the ice. That's the extent of my expertise."

She giggles. "Well, you could always show up to a practice and announce you don't know anything about the sport. I'm sure there would be plenty of men willing to explain it to you."

"Oh, joy. I can't wait." I roll my eyes but laugh anyway.

Hey, this is my life. This is what I do. Nobody ever said it would be easy.

"So, you're committing to this? Finding a hockey player for your next book?"

I stick my tongue out at her and make my voice sound nasally. "Yes, Miss Hayley."

"And you're going to give it your all because you're Kitty fucking Valentine and that's what you do?"

It's not so easy to make a snarky response when she puts it that way. "Yes, I'm going to give it my

"She's well-trained." I hold up a bag. "Pho? I thought it might help."

"Oh, thank you. I was just wondering if I should get up and fix something."

"You should've told me you weren't feeling well." I set things up on the coffee table before going to the kitchen to get him something to drink.

"I don't do well with being taken care of. Besides, aren't guys supposed to be tough?"

Sometimes, it's too much effort to even hide an eye roll. This is one of those times. "Gimme a break. I know you can be stubborn, but that's a little much, even for you."

"Stubborn, huh?"

"I get to call you that when I bring life-saving food and set it up for you." I nod toward the dog. "And when I take valuable time from happy hour to walk your dog."

"Oh, you went out earlier?" He looks me up and down. "You do look nice."

Darn it, I wish he wouldn't hand out casual compliments like that. Back in the pre-kiss days, I would've made a snarky comment about how bad he must think I look the rest of the time.

I didn't put a ton of effort into my look for the evening since I knew I was going to get an earful and not much else.

Now? I have to turn my attention to the soup I'm pouring out for myself, so he won't see how flustered that tiny compliment made me.

"Thanks. Hayley approved. So did the guys who tried to pick us up."

A quick glance in his direction reveals his tightening jaw. So, maybe I shouldn't have added that part, but I can't help myself when the opportunity is right there in front of me. We haven't talked about that moment in the kitchen since things went south with Paxton, which is probably for the best.

Even if it leaves me with a ton of questions. I don't think I can be blamed for testing the waters, seeing where he stands.

"She shut them down though. She's good at that. Tons of practice." I can't leave the poor guy hanging when he's not feeling well.

"Yeah, I can see how she'd attract a lot of attention."

I wait, staring at him. When he doesn't continue, I arch an eyebrow. "And?"

"And what?"

"What am I, chopped liver?"

"Nope. You're not going to trick me into giving you a compliment."

"I didn't know I needed to trick you." I wave an arm, indicating the soup and multiple containers of toppings and proteins. "Look at all the trouble I went to, and you can't even give me a teeny compliment?"

"I already told you, you look nice. I'm a one-compliment-per-night sort of guy." He takes a noisy slurp of his soup, which is heavy on jalapeños and

Sriracha. "And thank you for this."

I toss him a tissue box since nobody's sinuses can stay packed after all that heat. "So, tell me, how long have you felt sick?"

"A few days, I guess. I have plenty of sick and vacation time banked, so it's been easy to lose track of which day it is."

When he mentions that, I can't help but think about the weeks I've spent not working. It was one thing when Maggie forced me into a short sabbatical, but this has been ridiculous. I haven't been able to talk about it with Matt either since I haven't wanted to explain just why I've been unwilling to date somebody new.

Sure, I could use Paxton as an excuse with Matt since, of all people, he knows how betrayed I felt. But it's one thing to tell a fib based in reality over the phone or through email when I'm talking with Maggie. It's a whole other story when I have to lie to somebody's face—especially when they are part of the lie, whether they know it or not.

"It's easy to lose track of time when you aren't working," I reply. Settling for a vague answer.

"And when you feel like you'll never be able to breathe through your nose again. Colds are the worst." He blows his nose noisily, as if punctuating that statement.

"And here I was, thinking you were avoiding me."

"No, nothing as dramatic as that. Though

you've been quiet lately too. I figured you were busy, working on the next book."

Why does everything with Matt feel like it's so much more important now? Like everything has extra meaning, deeper significance? Back in the day, I would've happily talked about my work. If not happily, eagerly. Openly. I wouldn't have felt this twinge of awkwardness, wishing he hadn't mentioned it.

"Well, I haven't started the next book yet." I swirl the noodles around in my bowl before taking a mouthful. Chewing is easier than talking.

"You haven't? What's going on? I mean, I thought it was weird for you to not mention it, but …"

"Honestly, I'm tired. Tired of dating and writing about tropes. I miss the days when I could just write what I wanted. Sweet romances that filled readers' hearts with joy. You once asked if it was worth it, and I said it was. That I was happy to be getting out and meeting new people, but I'm not sure my emotions can take this roller-coaster ride for much longer."

"That makes sense. Honestly, I give you credit for not throwing in the towel after that last debacle."

"Yeah, that was bad. Of all the guys, that one hurt the most. But I'm tough." I flex a bicep for good measure, grunting.

He only shakes his head, snickering at me.

"Whatever you say, Valentine. But you can't break your contract either."

"This is true, which is why I really need to start on the next project. That's why I went to happy hour with Hayley. We picked the next trope."

"You sound unhappy."

"Not unhappy. Just not looking forward to having to learn about hockey."

To my surprise, his eyes light up. "It's a hockey book? I know all about hockey. I love hockey. Did I ever tell you I used to play?"

"No, you didn't. I had no idea."

"I'm sure you've heard me yelling at the games over here before."

"I've heard yelling, yeah, but I never knew what you were yelling at."

"So, what, you don't know anything about the sport?"

"I know there's a puck and ice involved."

"Well, that's a start." A smile plays over his lips as he picks up the remote and flips on the TV. It's hooked up to the internet, so it takes no time for him to pull up videos from various games.

"I didn't mean for this to turn into a lesson."

"I don't mind—unless you have something else you would rather be doing."

The sad part is, I don't. Even though he's sick and I'm deliberately keeping my distance and even though spending time with him isn't so great for my mental health since all I can do is question everything that comes out of his mouth anymore, I would still rather be here than across the hall, staring at a blank page on a computer screen.

"Well, if you think you're up to it."

The next thing I know, we're watching snippets of one game after another with Matt explaining the technique and skill behind what looks to me like a bunch of guys batting a puck around on the ice.

"When do they start fighting?"

He laughs, which unfortunately turns into a coughing fit. "You do realize, fighting isn't actually part of the game, right?" he asks after he can breathe again.

"Of course, but isn't it always more interesting when they do?"

It's like they heard me somehow. Suddenly, two players start throwing fists, and the crowd absolutely loses their mind while referees do their best to break things up. By the time it's finished, I'm wincing.

I'm supposed to date somebody who might be involved in something like that? I'm not sure my heart could handle it. *Do I really have to even date a hockey player? Maybe we could just be friends and hang out, and I could interview players. I mean, sex is sex. I can come up with that, right?*

Noticing my pensive look, Matt turns to me. "I'm sure whoever you end up with, he will be more than happy to explain the finer points to you."

I glance at him from the corner of my eye, unsure of whether there is a deeper meaning to what he just said. Oh, to go back to the days of being able to assume he was being snarky and not having to give it any further thought.

"I'm sure. Though honestly, I'm at my wits' end, trying to figure out how to meet a hockey player. What am I supposed to do? Put an ad in the newspaper? Or online somewhere? *Wanted: one hockey player who won't mind his life being used fictitiously in a romance novel.* Maybe that's how I should've approached this all along. It might've been easier."

"Probably, though can you imagine the sort of responses you would get?"

I shiver, remembering the copious amounts of unsolicited dick pics I got when asking if anyone knew an actor.

"Hey, didn't you find that doctor you dated on a site?"

"While I found some doctor potentials on that site, that's not how I met Jake. You should remember." I hold up the ankle I sprained, thanks to Phoebe tripping me on the stairs.

"Oh, right. That was the day I was sure the nurses at the hospital thought I'd hurt you." He rubs his temples, grimacing. "How could I forget?"

"I have no idea, but thanks for taking care of me." I quickly look away before he thinks my comment is more than a simple thank-you.

When my phone rings, the sight of my grandmother's name on the screen makes my hands tremble. Ever since her heart attack, I freak out a little whenever I get a call from her home number. Grandmother prefers we have our lengthy conversations in person, so I can't help but be nervous when I see her number appear on my phone.

"I realize we are a few days out from our normal weekly tea, but would you mind stopping in tomorrow afternoon?" The sound of her voice—confident, strident, full of energy—helps me breathe easier.

That's unexpected. The woman is nothing if not a stickler for routine. "Is everything okay?"

"Why is that the first thing you ask?"

"Because you're a creature of habit, and I literally can't remember the last time you called an unscheduled visit because it's probably never happened."

"Are you complaining?"

"Of course not. I'll be there. But you can't blame me for being concerned."

She clicks her tongue, chuckling. It seems like ever since she got together with Peter, her former longtime butler, she's become a different person. Sure, she can be sharp and dismayingly judgmental, and she has very definite opinions about my life and how I choose to live it, but there's a brightness to her now that wasn't there before. She can laugh at herself and at life, which I never thought was possible for her.

"I'll see you tomorrow, dear."

"Good-bye, Grandmother," I say before setting my phone down.

"Why did you immediately assume there was a bad reason for her to want to get together tomorrow?" Matt asks after I've ended the call.

"We're talking about a woman in her mid-seventies with a bad heart."

"You're a pessimist."

"I prefer to be called a realist."

"Yet here you are, writing about romance for a living. There's got to be some sort of hopeful spark alive in you."

Is there? I'm starting to wonder.

"Listen"—he finishes his soup before leaning back against the couch cushions, like he's exhausted from the effort of sitting up to eat—"I used to play in college. I decided not to go pro, but I keep in touch with some of the guys."

"Really? Do you think—"

"If I didn't think, I wouldn't have brought it up." He offers a tired smile. "I might be able to arrange taking you to a practice."

"You would do that?"

"What, we're friends, right? Of course I would do that. Give me a day or two to set it up."

And that's that. Once again, he's going to step in and help save the day. I only wish I didn't feel a strange sense of guilt for bringing him into it at all.

But Hayley's right, as always. I am Kitty fucking

Valentine, and I'm not going to let any man get in the way of my work. Especially when I now know we're *friends.*

Chapter Three

THE SECOND I see my grandmother's smiling face and the sly sparkle in her eye, I know something is up. But I also know better than to come straight out and ask her since she'll insist on asking why anything has to be up in the first place.

She wants to have some fun? I can have fun too.

"Any of those yummy cherry preserves left from the last time I was here? It was delicious on a scone." I'm very deliberate in fixing my tea just so, acting like this is any ordinary visit. I'm not going to give her the satisfaction of drooling over whatever news she has for me.

She sounds stiff when she answers, "No scones or preserves this time around, I'm afraid."

"Darn it. I wouldn't have come if I had known that."

"Kathryn."

"Okay, fine. It's nice, seeing you."

"You're full of sass today."

"What can I say? I try to get all of my sass out over the course of the week between our teas. There hasn't been enough time yet."

Finally, I can't help it. She looks like she's just about ready to burst out of her Chanel suit; she's so full of energy. It's cruel to keep her hanging like this. "So, what's with the last-minute invitation? It's obvious you're just dying to tell me."

She lifts her chin. "I am not dying to tell you."

"You don't have to act so insulted." I dunk a shortbread cookie into my tea, watching her as I do. "So? Spill."

"I'm getting married."

And there goes the cookie, straight into my cup. "You're what? Are you kidding? What—how—what—"

"Don't forget to breathe, dear." She can sound as dry and sarcastic as she wants, but there is absolutely no hiding the complete joy shining from her smile, her eyes. "Yes, Peter and I have decided to make things official."

I can barely place the cup on its saucer before I'm on my feet. "Where is he? How come he didn't tell me he was planning on asking?"

She waves this off. "He's visiting his nephew at the moment, to share the news."

"Hug me! Hug me already!" I have to yank her up from the sofa, but she's laughing by the time I throw my arms around her.

"I knew you would be glad." She looks suspiciously teary by the time I let her go.

"Glad? I'm freaking thrilled! Though if he thinks I'm going to get over him not coming to me for permission"—I wag a finger at her—"he's got another thing coming."

"To be honest, it was a mutual decision." She sits again, gesturing for me to do the same. "You've spoiled your tea. I'll pour a fresh cup."

Like I care about tea right now. My grandmother, who's been a widow for most of her life, is getting married. A woman who assured me more times than I could count that she didn't need a man, except for when her bed felt cold—and yes, she actually used those words once, and yes, I never quite got over it—is tying the knot.

"So, he didn't pop the question? You popped it?" Not that I would put it past her.

She might be old school, but that doesn't mean she carries an old-school mentality.

"To be honest, I don't remember exactly how we ended up on the subject. We might have easily started talking about the weather or the price of steak. Somehow, we ended up talking about marriage." She grins, and for a second, I swear, fifty years have melted away. "Come to think of it, I'm the one who suggested we go through with it."

"Ooh, go through with it. The romance is killing me."

"I hate to tell you, but life is often a lot less romantic than it is in the books you write."

I point to myself, eyes wide. "You're telling me this? Have we met?"

"A fair point."

"Okay, so you suggested you two go through with it. Once the thrill of romance and excitement died down, what happened?"

She shakes her head with a snicker. "You know him. I could tell he liked the idea of marriage a great deal, but he was hesitant."

"He's worried what people will think, isn't he?"

"To put it mildly. He doesn't want people to assume he's marrying me for my money."

"He only feels that way because he loves you so much."

I've already had these discussions with him, away from my grandmother. He worries about how her peers look at her, about the gossip their being together stirs up among the upper-crust idiots in her world.

Not that she hasn't already made it very clear what she thinks about their opinions. Not that she hasn't already cut some toxic people out of her life, thanks to him. If anything though, that's struck him as even more reason why he is no good for her. Causing her to alienate people who've been part of her life for decades.

Though seriously, it was the best thing she could've done, and she's happier for it.

"The man has spent years taking care of you, looking out for your best interests. You can't expect him to give up on that so easily."

"He thinks he knows what's best for me. That's the real problem."

I tap my chin, eyes turned upward. "Hmm. Who does that sound like?"

"Kathryn …"

"No, it doesn't sound like me. Let me keep thinking."

She blows out an exasperated sigh. "Regardless, I set him straight on that. I know what I want, and I know how long it has taken for me to find it."

I can't joke around anymore, not when she's so serious. I lean forward, a little choked up. "You're really happy, aren't you?"

She can try to hide her shy smile all she wants, but it's useless. Even though she's looking down at her teacup, I can see the way her ever-crimson mouth works upward at the corners. "Yes, I suppose I am. It's been so long since I've known happiness like this. I'm not ashamed to tell you, there are times when I ask myself if it can possibly be real."

"Well, the man has been with you for years, and he wants to stick around, so I think that's a good place to start."

"Yes, I suppose you're right about that."

I clap my hands together, eagerly rubbing them. "So, does this mean a big wedding? I'm seeing something lavish, maybe at The St. Regis or someplace like that."

"Oh, I haven't thought that far ahead. I called you nearly as soon as we decided."

I can't help it. I'm touched. "Really?" I ask, one

hand over my chest.

"Naturally. I couldn't think of anyone I would rather call than you. Though it did seem the sort of thing that ought to be announced in person."

"That means so much."

I know better by now than to think she would agree with my show of emotion. "Now, now. How many grandchildren do you think I have? And I would hope that if such a thing were to happen to you, you would call me first as well. Though I suppose you would want to reach out to Hayley first."

"I will call you right away. How does that sound?"

She likes to pretend she's beyond sentimentality, but I know better. There's a look of genuine happiness in her smile. "That sounds fair."

"Please tell me I can help you plan. I'll never have an opportunity like this again."

"You mean to tell me you don't think you'll ever plan your own wedding?"

"I don't mean it that way. I'll never have the chance to plan a wedding with so many resources at my disposal. Does that sound right? Or do I sound greedy?"

"Are you certain of that?"

"Certain of what?"

"Never having the opportunity again with abundant resources."

"Let's not even get started on that." If she can be

stubborn, so can I, and I've never liked the morbid game she plays where she reminds me of all the money she'll leave me in her will someday.

Besides, she'll be married now. There will be somebody else to leave her wealth to when she's gone.

But I don't want to think about that now. Or ever.

Good thing the front door opens, and Peter comes in, distracting me. The poor man looks downright horrified as I run to him, but he starts laughing when I throw my arms around his neck.

"I'm so, so happy."

"I hoped you would be."

"How could I not be?" I'm in tears by the time I let him go, but they're happy tears. Because he looks so overjoyed, so giddy almost. He's loved her for so long. "So, she finally talked you into it, huh?"

"Yes, somehow, she managed it. I have to admit, I'm a bit dazed still."

He takes a seat with us in the parlor, and Grandmother pours him a cup of tea. It's so fun, seeing the little things they do for each other without being asked—not to mention, how gratifying it is to watch her take care of him. It's usually the other way around.

"How did your nephew receive the news?"

"He seemed surprised, but pleased." He lets out a soft laugh. "I'm certain, for many years, he saw me as a permanent bachelor, so this is the last thing he expected."

This warms my heart, the two of them sitting shoulder to shoulder and smiling, and I wonder if second-chance romance is where my career needs to go. But I'm not sure if I could ever quite capture the beautiful charm of these two people who both imagined themselves beyond love, beyond romance and courtship.

There's something else weighing on my heart, too, something I'll keep to myself because the situation isn't about me.

But it's there, dragging me down, making it a struggle for me to keep smiling.

I want this. Plain and simple.

I'm tired of writing about people who find their true love while I bounce from one date to another, one boyfriend to another. I've been reaching out, hoping desperately that this will be *the one*. Paxton was about as close as I've ever come. I just feel this ever-present sense of yearning for something more. Something bigger. Something extraordinary.

I can't help it. I got into this business because I wanted to write about the sort of man I couldn't find in real life. Somebody wonderful, dependable, strong but loving. I'll always believe in romance—I mean, the evidence is right here in front of me, too obvious and too sweet to ignore.

I just need to start believing it's possible for me.

Chapter Four

"YOU'RE SURE YOU'RE feeling okay? You're up to this?"

Matt only laughs as we walk into the ice rink. "I had a cold, Kitty, and it's passed. I think I can handle watching a hockey practice."

"I'm just wondering, is all. You don't have to act like I'm an idiot for caring."

"You're not an idiot for caring."

I roll my eyes. "I'm just an idiot in general."

"No, I never said that. Jeez, woman, tone down the snark. I'm trying to help you."

We walk through the lobby, where the walls are covered in framed pictures of hockey players and skaters of all ages, and into the rink itself. Right away, I can see why he recommended I bring a sweater along.

Duh. There's ice in here. They have to keep it cold.

I untie the cardigan from around my waist and slide my arms into it as I ask myself if I should have brought a coat.

Too late now.

There are players on the ice, wearing pads and helmets, but they aren't skating with the kind of speed and urgency I saw in the videos Matt and I watched a few nights ago.

"What are they doing?"

"What does it look like to you?" For once, he doesn't sound snarky or like he's laughing at me.

"Like they're skating in circles around each other." I glance away from the skaters. "I mean, right? That's what it looks like. I expected them to work on … plays or something."

"Plays." He softens his snicker at least. I guess I should be grateful for that much. "Look closer. What are they doing with their sticks?"

I didn't know this was going to turn into a test. I have to squint from where we're standing at the top of a long, steep flight of stairs.

"Do I need glasses? Because I don't see—" I stop speaking as soon as I see it. The puck sliding back and forth between their sticks. "Whoa! They're passing it so fast! I can barely see their sticks moving."

"That's the point. They don't want to broadcast their pass. The less motion they can use while moving the puck back and forth, the better." He points to one of the players. "That's Luke Costello. I was always grateful he was on my team rather than playing against me. He's like the wind out there."

"Like the wind?" I have to smile. "I thought I was the writer."

"Shut up. You know what I mean."

I do, and he's right. It's not hyperbole. The player he's talking about, the one with the number 15 on his jersey, is insanely fast and smooth out there. He catches the puck—*catches? Is that even the right word?*—like it's nothing, like he'd expected it to be just where he was at the exact moment he glided past another player.

"Jeez." I can only shake my head in amazement. "There's not a chance that I could balance and pass a puck with a stick while moving. I took Bryce down when he thought I was being all cute about not being able to skate. He didn't believe me, but I showed him that I could not in fact skate. Who knows? He might still have the bruise to prove it." I chuckle.

"Oh, I would have believed you. I'm not always confident that you'll be able to sit up on the roof without somehow falling over the edge."

"You're lucky I've never pushed you over the ledge."

He only laughs as he starts down the stairs. People are sitting down in the first rows, sort of scattered around for the most part, except for a couple cluster of girls—one sitting at the end, the other behind a net.

A girl turns around to talk to somebody behind her, and that's when all hell breaks loose.

"Matty!" It's an ear-splitting squeal that gets the attention of the rest of the girls nearby.

"*Matty?*" I give him a look, brows raised, while a half-dozen girls—at least—spring up and come running like a rock star just entered the rink.

He ignores me, though I know him well enough to know he's pretending. There's a stiffness to him as he responds to the … enthusiastic greeting he's receiving.

A little too enthusiastic for my taste, but what do I know? Just because I find the act of falling all over a guy to be annoying doesn't mean there's anything wrong with this particular group hanging off Matt like he's the Second Coming.

"Where've you been?" The one who squealed his name at roughly the pitch of a dog whistle manages to stop squeezing him long enough to stare adoringly up at him. She's cute in a sporty kind of way, wearing an oversize jersey that reaches her knees with her long, dark hair flowing out from under a matching ball cap. It makes her look like a kid dressing up in adult clothes.

"You know, living life. Working." He waves at a few of the other girls. "There's more to life than hockey, Gin."

"Tell that to Mark. He'll drag you out with us after practice whether you want to come or not." She finally looks around him, finding me. "Oh, sorry. I didn't mean to ignore you. It's just that it's been such a long time since we've seen Matty."

"Yeah, Matty's been buried under his laptop for a while." I flash a wide smile his way and hope he doesn't think I'm going to let this go anytime soon. Because I'm not.

His smile is more of a grimace. I can practically hear his teeth grinding. "Ginger, this is Kitty Valentine. She's my neighbor, and she's an author, looking to write about hockey players for her next book."

"Ginger Grant." She shakes my hand. Firm grip.

I can already tell she's the queen bee of the group, the one who runs their circle. Who decides where they're going after every practice, after every game. She's the coordinator.

"It's good to meet you." I glance from her to Matt and back again. "So, are you here to support one of the players?"

She turns, pointing to the number on the back of her jersey. "Number 12. Mark Vance."

"Your boyfriend?"

She holds up her left hand, where a diamond sparkles. "Fiancé."

"No shit? I didn't know you two got engaged." Matt sounds unusually happy when he says this, and I'm not sure why. But I do know that I like this Ginger more now that I know this information.

The two of them chat over the specifics of how and when the proposal happened while I look over the girls now settling back into their seats after practically dancing with joy at the sight of the great Matt Ryder. A few of them are wearing jerseys, too, with the number of their guy on the back.

And they're just as interested in me as I am in them. I notice their glances toward me and then each other, which tells me they're wondering who I am and why I'm with good old Matty.

Ginger walks down the stairs, closer to the ice, and waves her arms to get someone's attention. Her fiancé, I guess.

Now that we're somewhat alone, I mutter, "My, aren't you a celebrity today, *Matty*?"

"Stop. It's just my old teammates and some girls. I'm hardly a celebrity."

I shoot him a skeptical look.

"I'm not. When I used to play, we were a tight group. After I decided not to go pro, I came to a few practices, but you know how it goes. Life happens." When that's not good enough and I keep staring at him, he shrugs. "What do you want me to say? This was a bigger part of my life at one point, but that's over now. I've moved on."

This is a sore spot for him. It's obvious, no matter how he tries to hide it.

"You never even told me before now that you played."

"Because it's not my life anymore."

He waves to one of the players who skated up to the glass, and I can see the *12* on his jersey. So, this is Ginger's fiancé. A few of the others break away from their practice and come on over to say hi.

Not the guy Matt pointed out to me though. Number 15. He's still out there, gliding around, passing the puck back and forth to himself. He's too focused to care much about what's going on away from the ice.

One of the girlfriends—I assume they're all girlfriends—catches me looking out in his direction. "A bomb could go off in this place, and Luke would keep skating. He's the most focused person I've ever met."

"He's very good. I mean, from what little I've seen of him, he seems good."

"He's a star." She joins me in watching him float over the ice. "He'll be the first to get called up from this team. I'd bet anything."

It would be rude of me to ask if he's single, wouldn't it? Yeah, probably, and for once, I'm going to think twice before letting curiosity get the better of me.

Instead, I observe the girls. Nobody's wearing his jersey, which seems like a good sign. *Did Matt point him out as a good candidate for my next book or just because he's a great player?*

"You're a writer?"

"Hmm? Oh, yes." I have to pry my eyes away from Luke to even pay attention to her question. It's like he's floating. I can't stop watching him purely because of his talent.

"What do you write about? Anything I've read?"

"Is the name Kitty Valentine familiar?" When she looks more confused than anything else, I have to grin. "Then, no, I don't think you've read anything I've written. I write romance."

Her eyes light up. "That must be so much fun!"

"Yes, it can be, but it's a lot of work. And depending on my character's background, a lot of research."

Before she can respond, Matt walks up behind me. "Hey, practice is about to wrap up, and I get the feeling I'd be handcuffed and dragged to the bar even if I said I didn't want to go out with the team." He lifts his brow. "You interested?"

I take a quick glance at Luke, who is still skating.

Yes, I'm interested.

If only to find out how a person manages to skate on thin blades while remembering how to play a game at the same time. I'd be a goner in seconds.

"Sure." I lift a shoulder like it's not that important either way, but he knows better. I can tell from the gleam in his eyes before he turns away.

And I sure as heck hope he didn't just set me up for an uncomfortable night. But I've seen that look in his eyes too many times to hope for anything else.

Chapter Five

IT'S OBVIOUS FROM the second we walk into the bar that this is where the team always gets together. They practically own the place, striding in casually, calling out to the bartenders and servers by their first names. The people tending bar start pouring beers right away without asking who wants what. I guess they know by now.

I can't help but feel like a fly on the wall, observing how the team members and their girls interact with each other. The guys acknowledge their girls in passing—a kiss, a pat on the butt, something—but for the most part, the players stick to themselves, and the girls maintain their cluster.

"Is it always like this?" I turn to the girl I talked to at the rink, whose name is Darcy. "Boys on one side, girls on the other?"

She nods, looking across the room to her boyfriend. I think his name is Bobby, but I haven't gotten many proper introductions. Besides, there are so many people on the team; there's no way I'd get everybody's name right on the first try.

"Yeah, this is the way it usually goes. When the

team's together, they talk about nothing but sports. Not just hockey either. If there's a game on TV, they wanna watch it. Or they'll talk about this week's football or baseball or whatever game is being played."

"Wow. Sounds super fun."

She giggles, and I decide I like her. She's friendly and approachable. Ginger, on the other hand, intimidates me a bit. I wish I knew why.

"Yeah, it gets boring real quick. So, we hang out and talk about what we wanna talk about, which of course, the guys think is all about periods and stuff, so they stay far away."

I have to laugh with her over that one. "Let them keep thinking it. That's how we ladies will end up ruling the world one day, making plans they're too scared to learn about."

"Amen."

We touch pint glasses and laugh some more. If anything, this is turning into a more enjoyable night than I first imagined.

Though Luke hasn't shown up yet. *Has he even left the ice?* Thinking back to what I witnessed earlier, maybe not.

There are ways I can find out what I want to know though. "So, are all the guys on the team dating somebody? It seems like an even one-to-one ratio."

"I guess writers observe all sorts of stuff, huh?"

"Now, I feel awkward."

"Don't." She touches my arm in a friendly, warm sort of way. "Most everyone on the team has a girlfriend at least. Greg and Mike are both married. Mark and Ginger just got engaged. The rest of us are girlfriends."

"Is there … how do I ask this … a high turnover rate?"

She just about chokes on her beer until I pat her on the back, feeling a little guilty. When I apologize, she shakes her head and giggles. "No, it's just … I've never heard it put that way before. I love it. A high turnover rate. And there is, but here's the thing: random girlfriends, dates, whatever—they don't come to practices. They might show for a game, but to sit through practices and whatnot? That means a girl has, like, passed a test or something."

"I think I understand what you mean."

To be a girlfriend to these guys, one has to devote her free time to his career—or what will, hopefully one day, be his career. I'm already taking notes in my head.

Darcy jerks her chin over my shoulder, toward the door. "Here comes Luke. I'll wave him over."

"Oh no, you don't have to do that." I swat my hand at her.

"Please. Don't play. You've been waiting to meet him ever since you saw him skate." When my eyes go wide, she grins. "You're not the only one who pays attention to things. You don't have to be a writer to be a girl who understands other girls."

I blush in embarrassment, but I decide I'm not stupid enough to actually keep her from waving him over.

Just as she's about to call his name, Matt comes up behind us. I lost track of him as soon as we entered the bar.

"There you are. Luke just came in. Do you want to meet him?"

"Sure." I sort of wish he weren't standing right here though. How's a girl supposed to get her flirt on when the neighbor who kissed her is standing right next to her?

I look over my shoulder in time to see Luke's ear-to-ear smile when he catches sight of Matt. He's tall, well-built—the way an athlete of his talent needs to be—with sandy-blond hair in a high-and-tight cut and a short, well-groomed beard. He's handsome, for sure, though his nose looks suspiciously like it's been broken at least once.

It's his bright, easygoing smile that catches my attention though when he reaches us. The smile of somebody completely at home in their skin. Confident, calm, sure of himself—on and off the ice. Unless my writer's imagination is running away with me, I think he's the sort of guy I wouldn't mind getting to know.

He claps Matt on the back before pulling him in for a bro hug. "Wow, man, it's been way too long! Don't tell me you're ready to put your skates on again."

Matt shakes his head with a laugh. "Nah. I'd much rather spend all my time messing around with numbers while you guys strap on your pads."

"Good. More room on the ice without your ego in the way."

Darcy bursts out laughing. "Sorry, don't mean to butt in, but look who's talking about an ego."

"Love you too." He turns his attention to me. "And who's this? Another new girl, Matt?"

Well, talk about an intro. My cheeks turn bright red as my gaze darts over to the man in question. I guess being a fabulous hockey player doesn't make a person exempt from putting their foot in their mouth.

Though how could he know?

And hang on a second. Did he say another?

None of your business, Kitty. I need to keep reminding myself of that.

"No, she's not that lucky." Matt smirks at me while I do everything in my power not to stick my tongue out at him. I'm trying to go for a good first impression here. "Luke, this is Kitty Valentine. She is lucky enough to live across the hall from me, and she's writing her latest romance novel about a hockey player."

"And he's left me with nothing to tell you about myself, so I'll settle for telling you that I think you're a hell of a skater." I hold out my hand, which he takes and squeezes in a firm shake.

"And that makes you my new favorite person." He winks at Matt before accepting a beer from one of the other guys on the team. "You've been hiding her from me, huh? I guess I can understand that."

Something flashes across Matt's face, something I've never seen before. Lord knows I've seen just about everything from him over time. Usually laughter at my expense, but there's been a lot more than that.

And this looks a heck of a lot like anger.

But it's gone in no time, replaced by a smug look I've definitely seen in the past. This I'm familiar with. "Maybe I was keeping her away from you for your own good. She's a walking disaster."

"Wow. Okay, thanks for talking me up." I shoot him a look while laughing a little too hard. "Maybe I should take the reins now."

"I think that's a good idea." Luke takes me by the hand, pulling me off my chair. "Let's find a quiet corner. If Ryder's so protective of you, that must make you worth getting to know."

Protective? That's what he calls it? I can think of a few better words, some of which I might need to share with my dear neighbor once we're away from witnesses.

But I'm trying to be on my best behavior, right? And killing him in front of so many people would probably be frowned upon.

"I've got to ask you a question." I turn to Luke when we're as alone as we can be in a crowded bar, sitting together at the far corner of the scuffed walnut bar.

"Yes, I've had my nose broken. Twice." His smile is disarming.

"I'll make note of that, but that's not what I had in mind." Though I was right, which says good things about my observational skills. "I was wondering how many hours you spend every week in practice."

He strokes his beard, like he's actually thinking, not simply showing off his impressive facial hair. "I normally work out on the ice four or five hours a day. Less in the off-season."

"Every day?"

When my mouth continues to hang open, he laughs. "What? Is that weird?"

"No, not weird. Impressive. How do you fit that in with a job?"

"Well, I'm a hockey trainer by day, player by nights and weekends." He grins. "I can book my clients around my schedule, and it keeps me on the ice, so I can easily practice before and after work. I read a long time ago about the amount of time it takes to master something. Ten thousand hours."

"Sure, of course. So, you figured you would put your ten thousand hours in?"

He nods.

"How many years have you been working toward that number?"

"Ten? Twelve?"

"I think you've hit it by now—and the work

shows, for sure." I look around the bar, picking out the different players and their girls. "And from what I've heard, it's only a matter of time before you get called up."

I didn't expect him to look so uncomfortable. "Sorry. Did I say something wrong?"

He flashes a grin. "You'll think it's stupid."

"You don't know that."

"Superstitious then. I know I can be."

"Oh, I wasn't supposed to mention getting called up? Sorry." I cringe.

"It's okay. I'll just have to go home and burn a sage bundle and perform my salt-circle ritual." He can't finish with a straight face. "I don't actually do that. Anymore," he adds.

"Good to know." We share a laugh before I offer, "I would feel the same if somebody was like, *This next book is going to be a best seller.*"

"Right? Like, *Don't do me any favors, thanks.*" He eyes me up with a thoughtful look. "So, have you written any best sellers?"

"I don't want to brag."

"So, you have." His teasing smile makes me blush. "Good for you. I'm sitting here with a best-selling author."

"And I'm sitting here with a professional hockey player."

We raise our glasses in a toast, and I try to fight off the slight tingle that races through me when our eyes meet. His are about as intense as everything else about him, the color of slate and framed by thick lashes.

"Was Ryder telling the truth when he said you're writing about hockey for your next book?"

I'm not used to hearing Matt being referred to by his last name. Why has it never occurred to me that he has an entire life outside of what I've seen? Friends, a past, hobbies he's never talked about. Meanwhile, he knows just about everything there is to know about me.

Well, mostly. He doesn't know how guilty it makes me feel to sit here and laugh and flirt with this guy while he's somewhere in the same room.

"Yep, I am. I could use insight into the game, the strategy, what it's like to work so hard to be a professional athlete." I eye him up, brows raised. "You interested?"

"Could be. You interested in hanging out tomorrow?"

"Sure." Then, I have to ask, "At the rink?"

"No, away from the rink. Before I let anybody in on the specifics of how I train, I have to take them to dinner first. It's a rule."

"I wouldn't want you to break the rules."

At least he's charming and easy to get along with. I guess I can make the enormous sacrifice of going out with him. Just once. Just to see what he's all about.

Luke excuses himself to go talk to the guys, and I return to my seat next to Darcy for the remainder of the night. After a few winks and giggles with her, we join the rest of the ladies and compare dress-shopping horror stories and all other matters of women until Matt comes over to take me home.

I say good-bye to everyone and let him lead me out of the bar.

"So? You gonna thank me now or wait until later?" Matt's wearing his oh-so-smug grin as we step outside.

"Thank you for what? Making fun of me earlier? But seeing as how I have a date with Luke tomorrow, I guess I'll refrain from wiping that smirk off your face," I say, elbowing him in the ribs.

"Well, you're welcome," he says with a big grin.

He makes it so hard to like him sometimes.

Chapter Six

"I HAVE TO admit, when I imagined sitting here and discussing these matters with you, our positions were reversed."

I look up from the wedding magazine on my lap—Grandmother's a wonderful lady, and she's way more open-minded than a lot of her contemporaries, but she's not interested in the vision boards I might or might not have put together for her big day—to roll my eyes. "You imagined discussing my wedding with me?"

"Naturally. What grandmother doesn't imagine her granddaughter finding happiness and love?"

"I've never been a grandmother before, so I wouldn't know."

"Trust me then." She looks around at the stacks of magazines I hauled to her house with a hopeless laugh. "I had no idea there were so many of these publications in print."

"Right? Weddings are big business. Though when my time comes, I'm sparing a few trees and doing this virtually." I'd be sparing my back, too, since these magazines were heavy.

"Virtually," she scoffs. "So silly."

"It saves paper."

"Says an author."

"Who sells e-books. Sheesh." I flip through to another spread. "Ooh, how do you feel about a string orchestra? Maybe do a brunch reception if you're not interested in throwing a huge blowout?"

"You've clearly given this more attention than I have over the last few days."

"Of course." I close the magazine after folding down the page I left off on. "This is huge. It's your wedding. You've spent all this time waiting for someone special to come into your life, and what you and Peter have found together is worth celebrating. What's the point of celebrating if you're not going to give it serious consideration? Like, this is emblematic of your entire relationship and you're sharing it with the rest of the world."

"You speak like someone who's given this a great deal of thought."

"What girl hasn't?"

"Plenty, from what I understand. Aren't young women of this day and age supposed to be career-minded? Not so focused on marriage?"

"We're talking about a *wedding*, not the marriage." I offer a helpless shrug. "Hi, I write romance for a living. I've planned so many weddings in my books, it's crazy. And I will admit, I have gotten a few ideas about what I want for my own someday."

"What have you imagined?"

"How much time do you have?"

"Plenty." Her eyes twinkle. "Though I'm getting on in years, so you might want to get straight to the point."

"When I was younger, I used to imagine a lavish ceremony at St. Patrick's. Don't laugh!" I warn when it looks like she's about to do just that. "Hey, Mom was a big fan of *The Sound of Music*. It's not my fault that I took one look at that wedding scene where Maria walks down the aisle with the veil stretching out behind her and decided that was what I wanted."

"Oh, yes," she sighs softly, batting her eyelashes. "I certainly wouldn't have minded seeing Christopher Plummer waiting for me at the end of the aisle. I wouldn't mind it now, honestly."

"But I've gotten older and figured out that isn't what I'm interested in. I think something more sophisticated is in order. Smaller too. I don't know enough people to fill a cathedral." I can't help but laugh at myself. "How was I supposed to know back then that my closest coworker would be my laptop?"

"Certainly, you would want the white dress and veil." She arches an eyebrow to go along with her dry tone of voice.

"Put that eyebrow back in its place, thank you very much. Hardly anybody expects a bride to be a virgin nowadays."

"There weren't all that many back in my day

now that you mention it."

"So, yes, white dress, veil, that whole thing. But simple. Classy. Elegant."

She nods in approval. "That's precisely the sort of event I imagine for you. You'll certainly be able to afford whatever you want—I demand it. The sky is the limit. Nothing is too good for my granddaughter."

"I don't expect you to pay for it."

"I fully intend to do so."

"I don't want you to."

"I don't recall asking whether you wanted me to or not."

"If it means I have to do everything your way just because you're footing the bill, I would like to respectfully decline."

"You have so little faith in me, Kathryn."

The woman could use a history lesson centered around the fact that we lost touch for much of my adolescence, thanks to her need to control things. My mom didn't like it any more than I do.

It's only the memory of that lost time that keeps me from crossing into annoyance. "I think we got off track. I'm not engaged, and we're already arguing over my wedding. It's *your* wedding we should be talking about."

She chuckles while pouring a fresh cup of tea. "Yes, you're probably right. Let me explain something. When I married your grandfather ... oh, it was so lovely."

Her gaze takes on a sort of faraway quality as she glances at the painting of her late husband on the wall. It's been there for as long as I can remember. He passed away when my mom was just a girl, yet that painting still stands there.

"Like something out of a dream. Have I ever shown you the photos?"

"No. I'd have remembered that, for sure."

"I'll have to find the albums someday, if only to show you how a wedding is really done. And to remind you, I haven't always been an old woman." She pats her smooth cheek with a grin. The woman is practically ageless, I swear.

"I should hope to be such an old woman."

"As I was saying, my first wedding was a beautiful event. Lavish. We had five hundred guests. Your grandfather and I had twelve attendants each."

"Twelve!"

She nods. "We danced into the night. Feasted on oysters and chicken Kiev, drank champagne. There were enough flowers to entrance an entire colony of bees. Candlelight, crystal, the most beautiful music. It was magical."

When she sighs though, there's sadness to it. "You know I loved your grandfather. We've spoken of him. We've also spoken of his failings and faults. His weaknesses."

His gambling. Yes, we've talked about that too.

She clears her throat, sitting up straighter. "The

reason I've brought this up is to point out the difference between a lavish wedding and a magical marriage. I loved your grandfather, but our perfect ceremony and reception weren't a recipe for a perfect marriage. Or even a long-lasting one."

"You couldn't have known how little time you'd have with him."

She lifts a shoulder. "All the more reason to affirm my commitment to Peter now—while we're both alive and well and able to be happy together. And the more reason to eschew a lavish event. I've had that. I don't need it again."

"What about him? What does he need?"

It's like he's been listening in. Heck, maybe he has been. Maybe he sort of fell into the habit of eavesdropping through the years. Peter joins us with a plate of sandwiches. "What do I need? A marriage license and a band on my finger. Everything else is window dressing as far as I'm concerned."

Grandmother gives me a wry smiles. "If he had his way, we'd go to city hall this very day and get it over with."

Get it over with? "Careful. I might swoon."

Peter only laughs in an indulgent sort of way, gentle as he usually is. "The outcome is the same regardless. The next day, we'll be husband and wife. And the day after that and so on. How many people are fortunate enough to be that happy?"

Grandmother's practically glowing. I can't help

but feel silly, trying to push the idea of a big wedding when the two of them are clearly thrilled just to be sitting next to each other, holding hands.

And how lucky she is, to have found a man who seems totally uninterested in her wealth. I guess there was no other way for her to find a man who'd love her just for herself—ironic really since she's prickly, even on a good day.

But that was the way it needed to be. He loves her for herself. He's not some fortune hunter. He put in three decades, almost four, and he took wonderful care of her the entire time. I don't know how else he could've proven that he doesn't care about the money and social position.

With that in mind, I put the rest of the magazines aside. "Whatever you want, I'm behind it. Though seriously, I'd appreciate an invite."

"As if we wouldn't invite you." Grandmother rolls her eyes and looks at Peter. "I suppose we could open the guest list to include my only grandchild."

"Whatever you want, dear." He winks at me in that conspiratorial way he always has. Like the two of us are in on a secret, and aren't we lucky?

We are. We definitely are.

"Now, there's only one thing left to do," he continues, looking my way.

"What's that?" I'm thinking, picking out wedding bands or something like that.

"We have to find you someone who's suitable

marriage material."

Did I just consider myself lucky a few moments ago? Shouldn't I know better by now?

After just about choking on my tea, I manage to sputter, "No, thanks. I'll take care of that on my own one day. And I think the two of you are spending too much time together, so long as we're airing grievances."

Chapter Seven

I SHOULD'VE KNOWN this was the sort of place we would end up on our first date.

"Is this okay with you?" Luke pulls out a chair for me, one facing the row of TVs mounted on the wall of the sports bar.

There are different games, pregames, and post-games playing on each screen. Talk about information overload. I don't know where to look.

I decide to look at him since that's where I would be looking if we were in a more intimate setting.

"This is great." Sure, I might be gritting my teeth as I smile, but I'm trying to go with the flow.

A sports bar isn't exactly my idea of a fabulous date location, but the man's life seems to revolve around sports, so I shouldn't be surprised.

Though next time, I'm going to choose the location.

"I figured we could relax and just get to know each other here." He signals a server before sitting down, dazzling me with that easygoing smile of his. That smile alone is enough to make me forget a multitude of sins.

And his body helps with the rest. I've never considered myself shallow, obsessed with a man's looks, but let's face it. The man is jacked. And the V-neck T-shirt he's wearing doesn't leave much to the imagination, tight around the biceps and chest.

A chest I would love nothing more than to rest my head against and fall asleep. Preferably after doing fun things together.

"So, who's playing tonight?" The place is crowded, meaning there's probably a big game going on. Then again, what do I know? Some folks just love sports, any sports, and it doesn't matter if the games are high stakes or not.

"It's the playoffs."

"Baseball?" I take a glance at one of the screens to confirm this for myself.

"Hey, so you do know something about sports."

"Yes, I occasionally stick my head out of my cave."

"Okay, in all seriousness, what's it like to be a writer?" He leans in, arms folded on the table. There's a definite glow in his eyes, like he's really interested in the answer I'll give.

Once you've been in the game as long as I have, you learn the difference between people who genuinely want to know what your life is like and people who only want their idea of your life confirmed. Those are generally the same people who think writing romance is nothing but writing sex and drinking champagne and eating chocolates all day.

Now, listen, I'm a big fan of both champagne and chocolate, but that's not the whole of it.

With that in mind, I offer a rueful smile. "It's more work than people think it is."

He nods slowly. "I'm sure it is. Honestly, I've always admired people who can create an entire world out of thin air. I mean, you have to dream up every single character in your book, and then you have to do it again and again. I can't imagine what that must be like."

"A lot of people don't see it that way. They think it's all fun—and it can be. I mean, there are days when I really do feel like I'm working magic. When everything flows without too much effort—that's when you know you're on the right track, you know what I mean? When everything seems to happen almost effortlessly."

"Yeah, I do. I have great days, where every shot lines up perfectly, and then some days, it's a real grind, a struggle. There are times when I have to talk myself into even lacing up my skates. That's something I don't think many people understand. Nobody feels like getting up and doing their job every single day. Not even athletes."

"I guess that's even worse if you've been hurt, huh?"

Something glows behind his eyes, a spark of something new. Excitement maybe or maybe just the satisfaction of being understood without having to try too hard. "Exactly. And then if we can't play because we work too hard or get hurt, we're the ones to blame."

"Just like my fans could devour every single one of my books and tell me how much they love my writing, but God forbid I'm late on a deadline. All of a sudden, I'm no good."

He laughs, clapping his hands together. "You get it! Wow, for once, I've found someone who gets it."

Who wouldn't warm up under that sort of praise? "It looks like we have common ground even though our professions are so completely different."

"Seems like we do. I wonder what else we have in common."

His fingers brush over the back of my hand as he reaches for a menu, and I have to ignore the tingle that runs up from my wrist and all the way to my shoulder.

I'm not in this for a boyfriend. I'm not in this to fall in love. I'm doing this for work. If I happen to enjoy myself in the meantime, that's great, but I can't lose sight of the big picture. Not like I did before.

"So, what do you do for fun?" He glances up from the menu with a smile.

"Fun? What is that?"

"Come on. Don't tell me you don't get out and enjoy life."

"What about you, Mr. Practices Four Hours Every Day?"

He shakes his head, chuckling. "Nope. I asked you first. You don't get to turn the tables on me that quickly."

"Fine. I go out. Drinks with my best friend, that sort of thing, but I'm mostly busy with my work." He doesn't need to know about weeks spent idling around my apartment or going for endless walks in Central Park. Or the multiple men I've dated for the sake of my career. There are some things I'd prefer not to share.

"So, you don't go out all that much?"

I shake my head.

"And here we are, with something else in common."

"You're a driven person. You focus a lot of your energy on your goals. It's only natural."

His smile widens further. "Man, I should bring you around more often, so you can be my translator. I try to explain what you just said, but it never comes out the right way."

Our server brings us a couple of beers, and they go down way too easily. Now that we're talking and opening up, I like the fact that this is where he chose for us to have our first date. We're relaxed, and there isn't all of the unspoken expectations on either of our shoulders.

"So, let me guess." I look him up and down, stroking my chin the way he sometimes strokes his beard. "You get a lot of flak from people who don't understand why you spend so much time on the ice."

"You could describe it like that, yes." And the way he grimaces tells me it's a little more serious than that. "Though it's not just being on the ice. I'm training, working out, running. Everything's directed toward my ultimate goal."

His intensity isn't intimidating. In fact, it's sort of cute. Charming. Though nobody would ever refer to him as cute with a straight face. Hot, more like it.

"Who doesn't understand? Family? Friends?"

"Most of my friends are on the team, so it's my family more than anybody else. They're proud of me, and they want me to reach my goals, but they also don't want to see me get burned out, so my mom always harps on me to take enough breaks so that I won't overdo it." He turns his glass around and around on the table, his jaw tightening.

"For what it's worth, I get a lot of the same flak from my grandmother. She's my only living relative, so—"

He winces, his eyes meeting mine. "I'm sorry. I shouldn't be complaining."

"Of course you should! I mean, it's your life. This is your reality. Don't get the wrong idea. Just because my parents aren't with me anymore doesn't mean I can't relate to family pressure."

"Now, I feel like a real dick for complaining."

"Listen, I can complain about my grandmother until the cows come home. The woman can be impossible. But I love her. Besides, I don't think anything you said was complaining. You're frustrated, and you're sharing with somebody who can relate."

He looks me up and down. "I can't believe Ryder got lucky enough to have a neighbor like you. And I can't believe I got lucky enough that he brought you to practice."

"Let's get this straight. You got lucky that I ended up having to write about hockey players this time around." I give him a wink and a smirk before taking a sip from my beer.

"Okay, I see how it is." At least he's smiling again. "I hope this isn't all about that though."

"That remains to be seen." I'm trying to take a page out of my grandmother's book here, trying to seem playful yet distant and fully in control of the situation.

And it's working; I can tell. But he's an athlete, one who sets a goal for himself and goes nonstop to reach it.

Is he thinking about me as a goal? A goal to be achieved?

Do I want to be one?

There's a burst of noise, pulling our attention away from each other and toward the rowdy guys watching the game. One of them backs away from the TV, shouting profanity with a beer in one hand.

A beer that, naturally, he spills all over me.

I jump up, gasping, and luckily manage to avoid the worst of it. I end up with some of it on my jeans and blouse and reek of a brewery, but it's not the worst thing that's ever happened—hello, sprained ankle and skinned knees.

Clearly, Luke feels differently about things. "Yo, man! What the hell do you think you're doing? You realize you're not the only person here, right?"

If the beer spill didn't attract attention, his shouting definitely is.

"It's not that big of a deal—" I might as well not even be speaking.

I almost feel sorry for the guy, who is clearly half-drunk already and had no idea what he was doing when he stumbled against our table. Luke's a good head taller than him and a lot more muscular. This poor dude wouldn't stand a chance.

"Sorry, sorry," he mumbles and then hands me a wad of napkins. "I'm sorry."

"Accidents happen." I do everything I can to make the man feel better since it's obvious he's embarrassed. "Don't worry about it."

Once he moves off, I turn to Luke. He hasn't calmed down at all. "Really. I'm fine. He didn't mean to—"

"He should have been the one apologizing to you. Not the other way around." He's still glaring at the back of the man's head—a head which, I've noticed, is farther away than it was before. He's probably afraid of Luke.

Frankly, seeing how quickly his temper flared, I can't entirely blame the guy.

"And he did apologize." I do the best I can to mop up my clothes, and a server joins us and cleans up the table. "Sometimes, you just have to accept an apology and move on. And I didn't apologize to him."

"Don't let yourself get walked on. That's one thing I can't stand—when people walk over other people."

There's more noise surrounding the game, and I guess I could raise my voice over it, so he would hear me, but it doesn't seem worth it now. I'm not going to stand here and have an argument over this.

"You know what? This is really nice, but I think I want to go home and change into something that's dry."

His tone changes in a heartbeat. "Wait, don't leave because of this."

"I'm not." That's a lie. I'm definitely leaving because of this.

We were having a nice time until that happened. If he could've laughed it off or at least helped me clean up, things might've turned out differently.

I mean, I'm the one who stinks like hops and yeast. Not him.

"Can I see you home at least?" He quickly pays for our beers before following me out of the bar.

"I was going to walk. It's not very far." I don't

want to necessarily shut this down before I have a chance to learn about the sport, what it's like to be a player, and especially what it's like to date one.

And he does seem like a decent person—when he isn't flying into a temper tantrum.

We walk a block in silence with me asking myself whether this is a complete mistake. Work or no work, I'm not going to ignore red flags for the sake of my career. I ignored enough of them with Paxton, and I can see that now. I can't keep making the same mistakes again and again.

Luke's the first one to speak after crossing to the next block. "Can I tell you something? And you're free to say no if you don't want to hear anything from me after the jackass I just made of myself back there."

I look at him from the corner of my eye. "At least you can admit that."

"I know it was wrong, and I am truly sorry. It's not even so much the situation we were in at that moment that set me off. I'm not saying this to excuse myself since I should've handled it better. I wasn't even the person who had the beer spilled on them."

"That's true."

He's quiet for a second, too busy taking a deep breath before speaking, "I have a twin brother."

"Okay." Not sure what that has to do with anything, but I imagine he'll tell me.

"He's paralyzed from the waist down."

"Oh. I'm sorry to hear that."

"It hasn't been easy. The accident happened when we were kids. And ever since then, it's like our lives have gone on two different trajectories. But he's still my best friend. And he's exceptional in everything he does—he plays in a wheelchair basketball league, all kinds of things like that. But, there are a lot of ignorant people in the world. Especially when you're a kid—other kids can be cruel and thoughtless. There've been a lot of times when he was ignored, looked past, talked over. So many people in restaurants have tripped over his chair or banged into him from behind and spilled something on him."

I'm starting to understand why he's telling me this.

We stop at a red light, and he shoves his hands into the pockets of his jeans. His shoulders are up around his ears, his chin tucked in, like he's embarrassed. "You have no idea how many times I've wanted to hit somebody for what they did to him. He always handles it well. He's much more even-keeled than me, but I know it still bothers him."

"I really am sorry he has to go through that. People can be so thoughtless."

"I flashed to that when that guy got beer on you. There's no excuse for it. It's something I have to work on. I'm too protective of my brother, and that sort of spills over sometimes."

"No pun intended," I offer with a tiny smile.

I can see the relief written all over his face. "Yeah, no pun intended."

"I really do understand, and I'm glad you told me about your brother. Now, I don't have to wonder if you have anger management issues."

"No, I can't remember the last time I got into a fight off the ice."

I lift an eyebrow. "What about on the ice? Do you do a lot of that?"

"I try not to."

But I know by his sheepish grin that he does his share. Still, he doesn't strike me as someone who gets off on being violent, so I won't give him a hard time.

"I get it. I really do. But like I said, I'm fine. Sometimes, you have to let people fight their own battles too."

"I'm not very good at that. I'm always the one who tries to fix things for everybody. I guess that's what I do in my free time when I'm not on the ice."

I can tell that my laughter makes him feel better, and that makes me feel better. His heart was in the right place—at least, that's how it seems—and I can't hold it against him if he gets overly protective.

"This is me." I stop in front of the wide steps leading up to my front door.

His eyes widen. "No shit? Sorry, pardon my French."

"No shit."

He looks the building up and down with a smirk. "I had no idea Ryder lived in such a nice part of town. I have to give him shit about it the next time I see him."

Men are weird. Why would anybody make fun of a person for living in a nice part of town? It seemed like all of them did a lot of ball-busting when they were together, come to think of it.

"I would invite you up, but …" I offer a shrug.

"No, I wouldn't even think about it." When I narrow my eyes, he laughs. "Okay, I would think about it, but it's always up to you. Besides, it's not like the night ended very romantically, and that was my fault. I would like to make it up to you, if you'd let me."

"I think I could arrange that. What do you have in mind?"

He strokes his beard. "I have practice the next few nights actually."

No surprise there. "If you want to make it up to me, let me come to one of the practices."

"They're open. You can come anytime you want."

"I was led to believe only special girls make it to practices."

He winks before taking my hand. "And who says you're not special?"

I don't pull away when he leans in to kiss my cheek—quite the opposite in fact. It's sweet and gentle, and I can't help but have a good feeling about him as a person in spite of what happened at the bar.

Though I'm very glad there's no hope of this going anywhere just the same.

This is for work. Nothing more than that.

Chapter Eight

"I'M GLAD I thought to bring an actual jacket with me this time." I shove my arms into it, wrapping it around myself. "It's so cold in here."

Darcy nods, smirking. "Honestly, after a few hours in here, it's easy to forget what the weather is like outside. It's eternally winter at hockey practice." Her eyes dart back and forth, like she's making sure nobody's listening in on us. "So? How did your date go?"

"How did you even know—"

She waves a hand. "Please, there are no secrets on the team. He must've mentioned it to one of the guys, and word spreads fast. You know, they talk about us and make it sound like we're a bunch of gossip addicts, but they're just as bad."

"It sure sounds that way."

I guess it doesn't matter either way. Though I do have to keep in mind that men consider very few things off the table when they're together in that sort of environment. Especially once they hit the locker room.

With that in mind, I ask, "Do you ever feel self-conscious? Like you're worried your secrets will be spilled since they're all so close and share so much?"

Is it my imagination, or did her skin just go pale? Maybe it's the harsh fluorescent lights.

"I wasn't until now."

"I'm sorry! I'm sorry! I didn't mean anything by that. I'm just trying to get a sense of what it's like to seriously date one of these guys."

"I can tell you all about it." Ginger plops down in a seat in front of us. Of course she does. It's like she has a sixth sense. And she's been buzzing around all throughout practice, checking in on one group after another.

It has to be exhausting for her. She can't just sit and relax and watch her man play. Then again, how many practices can a girl sit through and actually pay full attention?

I have to play nice, so I pretend to be interested in what she has to offer. "I guess you guys have been together for a long time, huh?"

She counts on her fingers. "It'll be three years next month actually. And we got engaged last month."

"You come to every practice?"

She shakes her head, laughing. "God, no! I try to make one or two a week, just to show my support. I know it means a lot to him, like I have his back."

I turn to Darcy. "What about you?"

"One or two a week, maybe. And I try to make it

to every game, though sometimes, I have a ton of work to get through at home. I'm a teacher," she explains, and I raise my eyebrows.

"I'm sorry. I should've asked you before now. You know all about what I do, but I never asked what you do for a living."

She only giggles. "You sort of got stolen from me by a certain player."

Ginger nudges Darcy's knee. "I see you've even brought tests and papers with you to grade."

"That's true," Darcy admits. "I've brought work along to practices on more than one occasion. Sometimes, it's just too quiet at home when he's here."

"I usually work better with a bit of background noise too." I turn to Ginger again; if she insists on breaking into our conversation, I might as well learn what I can from her. "You said you know he likes to feel supported by you."

She flutters her very long, very dark lashes. I almost want to ask if she wears a full face of makeup to every practice she attends, but something tells me I already know the answer. Not that there's anything wrong with that, but it gives me an idea of how image-focused she is. "Sure, like what's important to him is important to me."

"I have to ask, is this reciprocated? Don't get me wrong; I'm not going to analyze your relationship. I'm wanting to develop my main character, my hero, and I'm trying to get ideas of what other athletes think and do and say."

Her mouth opens. Her mouth closes. "Now that you mention it, I've never really thought about it that way."

I flinch, feeling guilty for prying. "I'm sorry. I didn't mean—"

"No, no," she mumbles, waving her hands, staring off past Darcy and me. Like she's trying to think of something. "It's not that he doesn't care. But this is a huge part of his life. It was before I met him, and it always will be."

"I completely understand that. I was just explaining to Luke yesterday that—"

Her eyes light up, and she practically jumps on me. "How did it go? Did you two hit it off? Well, I guess you must have since you're here."

"Down, girl." Darcy doesn't look as amused as she's trying to make herself sound. In fact, she looks disgusted. "It's none of our business."

"You're right, of course," Ginger says, looking crestfallen.

"We didn't exactly *not* hit it off, if that helps." I wink, and she brightens up.

Somebody calls her name, which is a relief. Something tells me it's not just the players who are into gossip—I mean, am I not supposed to expect her to report to the other girls that Luke and I did go on a date and that it did go decently well? I have to make a mental note not to reveal too much in front of her—like, ever.

"Sorry about her." Darcy's watching the back of Ginger's head. She sighs. "She's cool and everything, but sometimes, she's a bit much. Especially when you don't know her and aren't, like, used to her."

"She immediately struck me as the queen bee of the group. Am I wrong about that?"

"Nope." She taps the tip of her nose. "I mean, it's not like we held an election or anything. She basically claimed the title for herself way back, years ago."

"When she started dating Mark, I'm guessing?"

To my surprise, she pulls an incredulous face and shakes her head. "No, she's been around longer than that."

It takes me a second. A long second, to be honest. "Oh! You mean, she dated someone else from the team?" I ask in a whisper since it seems like I might be on the verge of hearing some drama.

Her smile fades. She blinks, staring at me. "Okay, I thought you were kidding, but it's obvious you weren't. I figured he told you!"

"Luke? She dated Luke?" Oh, gross. I don't want to be the girl he rebounds to, though three years is a long rebound.

"No, Matt!"

And just like that, the needle scratches the record.

Say what now? "She dated Matt? Matt Ryder?" I manage to stop short of saying my Matt since he's not my Matt.

Her head bobs up and down. "I figured he would've mentioned something about it. It was a big deal. I probably shouldn't be the one to tell you about it. It was wrong of me to even bring it up, but I didn't know."

"No, it's okay. And you're right; we shouldn't say anything more about it. I'm sure he wouldn't appreciate it if he knew we were talking about it."

Matt and Ginger. Matt and Ginger? In what universe does that even make sense? She seems like the exact opposite of the kind of person he would date.

Then again, what the heck do I know? He's more and more of an enigma all the time. Just when I think I have him figured out, he throws me a curveball like this one.

Ginger. God, I can't imagine they wouldn't kill each other right off the bat. Their personalities are all wrong. And now, here's Darcy, telling me it was a big deal. I wish I hadn't stopped her.

"Can I tell you something else? It's not about her and Matt, when they were together."

"Okay …"

She practically whispers straight into my ear, "She must've asked every single person in the bar that night who you were and what was going on between you and Matt."

I knew it. She was way too interested in me, way too bright and bubbly when Matt walked into the rink. "I doubt anybody knew anything."

"No, they really didn't."

"Which makes sense since we're neighbors. He's just a friend doing another friend a favor."

"Well, she sure didn't see it that way. That's just how she is. It doesn't matter that she's engaged to Mark. She thinks that Matt is still hers."

Well, the girl has another thing coming if she thinks that's true. He might not be mine, but he's sure as hell not hers.

There's a rush of heat in my chest, in my head, and I have to take a slow breath in through my nose and out through my mouth, like I'm on my yoga mat. Luckily, I'm well practiced in yoga. My body immediately responds to the change in my breathing. It's like I've rewired my brain or something over the years.

And maybe once I get home and I have the chance to think it all over, I'll be able to figure out why I had that reaction in the first place.

It's not easy, getting through the rest of the night, asking questions and only half-listening to the answers. It's not easy, paying attention to the activity on the ice either, not when my gaze keeps hitting the back of Ginger's head over and over.

I wonder how long they dated. I wonder who ended it.

I wonder how long it took him to get over her.

Or if he's over her at all.

Chapter Nine

"OH MY GOD. Please tell me you didn't bring this up with him."

It's a miracle none of my eggs Benedict falls out of my mouth; Hayley surprises me so much. "Do I strike you as having lost my mind? Because, obviously, that's what would have to happen for me to ever bring this up with him."

"Good." She pretends to wipe sweat off her forehead before going back to her egg-white omelet. "It's none of your business."

"Why are you telling me that? I know that. Jeez, it's like you think I don't have any tact at all."

"No comment."

"Which is in and of itself a comment, and you know it very well."

"Whatever you say."

She knows how crazy it makes me when she acts like this, all blithe and innocent. Like I'm the one with a problem while all she's doing is sitting and eating her brunch.

"I wouldn't know how to approach it with him anyway even if I did bring it up. Which I won't," I add when she glares at me. "I'm sorry, but you don't think it's the slightest bit interesting?"

"Absolutely not."

"How can you say that?"

"Because it's the truth. So what if he dated her?"

"You don't get it."

"It's clear I don't." She puts down her knife and fork in favor of turning her full attention to me, and I sort of wish she hadn't. She's hitting me with that penetrating glare of hers, and it makes my skin crawl.

I heave a heavy sigh, very dramatic, though not even that can properly convey how mixed up I feel. "Obviously, things didn't go well."

"Obviously."

"And he feels like he can't or shouldn't say anything about his former relationship with Ginger."

"Or that he doesn't need to," she points out. "That's very possible too. Because he doesn't have to say anything. He doesn't owe you an explanation, and you don't owe him one for anybody you date either."

"I realize that. It's just that ... I don't know. It doesn't feel right." I ball up a fist and press it against my sternum. "In here. Something feels off in here."

"It could be gas."

"Oh my God."

She snorts. "Maybe you just want something to be off. Maybe you want there to be some drama you can jump into and involve yourself in."

I can't help but pout at the top of her head, which is all I can see as she digs back into her brunch. It's not Matt I'm pouting over either. "What did I do to make you mad at me?"

Her head snaps up. "I'm not mad at you."

"You're not in a good mood with me. How come? Did I do something wrong? Or is there something you want to tell me that I haven't given you the chance to tell me yet?"

Ever since I found out after the fact that she was dating somebody at work—somebody she should not have been dating—I've tried to be more aware of what's going on in her world. I can't imagine how difficult it is to be friends with me. I know I'm not a bad person, but I can be a little much. A little too dramatic, a little too wrapped up in my work and my personal drama.

The least I can do is try to be here for her if she needs me.

I can tell when she lifts a shoulder and spears a piece of turkey sausage without meeting my gaze that there is something going on. "Honestly, it doesn't have to do with you. I'm just in a mood."

"What is it? The whole point of us getting together when we can manage it is to talk things out, right? To keep up with each other? That's a two-way street, babe."

She offers a faint smile, but I can sense her hesitation. "You're right. I guess it's easier to sit and listen than to bring up my own problems. Not really problems. That's not what I mean." She puts her head in her hands, which is awkward since she's holding her silverware.

This is new. Hayley is probably the most confident, competent, put-together person I know. Seeing her like this is like seeing the Pope light up a cigarette and walk into a strip joint. It would never happen. At least, I hope not.

Yet here she is, looking more rattled than I've seen her since …

"Are you seeing somebody? Or thinking about it?"

From my vantage point, I can see her forehead crinkle, and I know I've hit a nerve. "If I was?"

"Well, I would hope he was the right person for you. I would hope you were happy. I would hope there weren't any complications." I have to tread carefully around that one since I don't want her thinking I'm harping on her for past mistakes.

"We're already seeing each other." She finally drops her hands, deflating. "Sort of. Sleeping together when we can. I don't even know if he wants to see me more seriously. I don't know if he thinks about me that way."

"Hayley, wake up. You know how dazzling you are. You have to."

"It's not about that. I know I could probably hook up with just about anybody I set my sights on. I'm not trying to brag."

"Trust me, I get it."

"But this isn't like that. He's … interesting. Fascinating. We can just sit and talk for ages."

"So, it is someone from work." I try to keep my expression neutral along with my tone of voice. I don't want her thinking I'm getting judgmental.

"He flew in from the LA office a couple of weeks ago. Another associate, just like me, not a boss or an assistant. We're on the same level."

"Well, that's good."

"And he's just … awesome." This time, she covers her face with her hands, but at least her hands are empty now.

I can hear her giggling from behind her palms. It makes me giggle too. "Are you serious? You're smitten with him!"

"Honestly?" She peeks at me from between two fingers. "I don't think I've felt this way about anybody since college. Like that giddy, breathless feeling. Like I'm always super aware of where he is, what he's doing. When I hear his voice out in the hallway, coming my way, my heart skips a beat, and I don't know what to do. I get all flustered, but I'm also so happy because he's there."

"You realize this is totally adorable, right?"

She groans, throwing her head back. "It doesn't feel adorable."

"How does it feel?"

She waves her hands around, trying to find a word. "Confusing. Mixed up. Concerning."

"Why concerning?"

"This is me! I don't get this way over men. Not ever. If I like somebody, I find out if he likes me, and I go for it. Granted, it's been a while, but that's how it used to go."

I have to sit back and think this over. We've known each other a long time, and I've seen her date quite a few men over the years. She literally has her pick of anybody she wants, being the total package she is. Yet over the last several years, her focus has been solely on her career—and rightly so.

"I guess that means this one is special."

She blinks hard. "That's all you have for me? He's special? I know he's special. He's incredible and brilliant and funny and kind. He's everything I want, wrapped up in one delicious package."

"Boy, you have got it bad."

"Kitty ..." She only stops short of burying her head in her arms because of the plate in front of her. I can tell she wants to.

"This is actually fun. I get to be you in this conversation for once."

"Great. Maybe I'll get to be the one to say something to embarrass us in public this time."

"Okay, that's a hit below the belt."

Her face falls. "I just don't know what to do."

I have to admit, it takes me a second. Longer than a second. Longer than it should, for sure. "You really have feelings for him already. This isn't just a crush. You're falling for him—for real."

She looks down at the table, drawing invisible patterns with her finger. "Maybe. A little."

My heart sinks, though it shouldn't. But I can see where this has been going all along. "He'll have to go back to LA at some point, won't he?"

Her head slowly bobs up and down.

"And you don't know what will happen once the day comes."

Again, she nods, looking down at the table.

"And maybe you're kinda, sorta considering going out there with him."

"No." Her head pops up, eyes bright. "No, that's not what I want to do. This is where my life is. This is where my family is. This is where you are. I'm not going to move across the country."

"And what does he think? What's his name?"

"Nicholas. He knows he's going to have to go back eventually, and whenever I try to bring it up, he changes the subject. I finally asked why, and he told me it's because he doesn't want to think too far past today. He's very much that sort of person. He doesn't want to waste what we have today by worrying about tomorrow."

"I can understand that. Although …"

As usual, she reads my mind. "Trust me, I've done my homework. Some digging with the girls in the LA office. He really is single, and he even goes home regularly for Sunday dinner with his parents."

I let out a sigh and put one hand over my heart.

"That right there earns him points."

"I know, right? He's not one of those cutthroat types you see all the time in my business. He's smart, he's sharp, but he has integrity. I think that's what set him apart from the beginning. He always wants to do the right thing even if it means leaving some money on the table. He's even super precise when it comes to his billable hours. And when we're working, we're working, not talking about us or about anything else—even if it's not that easy to keep our minds on work all the time. It wouldn't be fair to the client otherwise."

"I like him."

"So do I. A lot."

So, why does she look so miserable? Staring down at her folded hands, chewing her lip.

"Hey. Look at me."

She does, though it takes a second for her to raise her head.

"Listen, all I want—all I ever want—is for you to be happy. For you to have what you need, what you want. And if you want him, then there's no reason why you shouldn't go for it."

"But—"

I shake my head, emphatic. "No buts. I'm serious. You deserve something for yourself. You've worked so hard, tirelessly. It's obvious Nicholas has woken up something else inside you, something else you need. None of this sort of stuff was important to you before you met him, and maybe that's because he's what you've been waiting for even if you didn't know you were waiting. Maybe you've finally found someone worthy of you."

"Great, and he just happens to live across the country."

"You want my advice?"

She nods.

"Don't turn away from this just because of surface problems. And that's all this is—a problem on the surface. Self-imposed limitation. Do you honestly think that if Nicholas wanted you to come out there with him, anybody in your life would slow you down or hold you back? If you were able to work out of that office instead of this one, here in New York, I would be the first person to help you pack."

She snickers. "Thanks."

"I mean it. I'm not kidding around. I would miss you like I'd miss my right arm, but I'd get over it because what I want more than anything is what's best for you. You need to feel fulfilled. And if this is part of what you need so you can feel fulfilled, I'm right here, cheering you on."

She wipes a tear from the corner of her eye with a sheepish smile. "I guess that's why I was in a mood. Because here you are, with Matt right in front of you, and you're still playing guessing games with yourself."

I try not to bristle at that since it sounds sort of dismissive, and I don't enjoy it very much. But I know she didn't mean anything negative by it. "Let me ask you something. If all the stars aligned and you were granted a transfer, and Nicholas invited you to move back to LA to be with him, and your family and everybody else was completely behind you, what would be standing in your way? Would you have any other hesitations?"

Understanding dawns in her eyes. "Yeah, of course. I would be worried about what would happen if things didn't work out. Could I just uproot my entire life, so I could be with somebody things might not work out with?"

"There you go. It's not exactly the same thing, but it's close. If things didn't work out between me and Matt, I don't think I could handle living across the hall from him. I would have to move. There are just too many feelings involved, you know? It would be like walking on eggshells for the rest of the time I stayed in my apartment and he stayed in his."

"I get it. I really do." She chews her lip before shrugging. "Well, I guess we both have to be brave, no? Sometimes, you have to put aside your fears and go for it. Otherwise, you could be missing out on something incredible."

She makes it sound so simple.

Chapter Ten

"ARE YOU SURE you wouldn't rather go out for drinks with the rest of the team?"

Luke shakes his head as we climb the stairs leading up into my building. "No way. I see too much of them as it is." He trails off with a bit of a chuckle, but I hear the truth in his words.

"I guess I should just consider myself lucky you have time to spend with me at all." I give him a grin as we start climbing to my floor.

"I know it's not easy, trying to date somebody like me."

"Remember, I'm probably the only person who fully understands what it's like to work so hard and have a schedule so unlike everybody else's."

"True."

"Well, at least you're doing a job you like. It plays to your strengths."

All he does is groan. "You should see some of the parents. I swear, if their kid didn't score the winning goal in the last game, they want to know how I failed."

I chuckle.

"I'm not kidding," he insists. "At first, I made the mistake of not including a disclaimer in my contract. I can only promise so much. And some of the kids … I'm sorry, but not everybody is meant to be an athlete."

"It makes me sad for those kids. They must want it so badly."

"Honestly, a lot of them don't. Which also puts me in an awkward position. I can't exactly go up to their parents and tell them their child has no desire to ever do this for the rest of their life. These poor kids want to please their parents so badly. But a lot of them, their hearts aren't in it."

"That really is sad."

"I know. But everybody needs to make a living too, right?" He groans, frustrated. "I can't wait until I get called up. If you want to know what drives me, that's a big part of it. The idea of not having to work a day job to make ends meet. Being able to give hockey my full attention." He sounds downright wistful, and I guess he is.

At least our conversation has given me something else to think about besides the nervous flutter in the pit of my stomach. He's coming to my place, which, of course, means I spent a good chunk of time today making sure everything was clean and tidy.

We'll be really and truly alone since we started seeing each other a week ago. Aside from that date at the bar, which ended abruptly, we've only gotten together under the context of practice and then meeting up with everybody afterward.

I'm fine with things being the way they are. We haven't rushed into any sort of physical relationship, and I'm okay with that too. I would rather take it slow, get to know each other, and fill in the sexy details later. Even if it means making things up for the sake of the book—and I've done that on more than one occasion—I can say that the real, important writing I'm doing is based in reality. The meat of the story, the thoughts and concerns and fears of an athlete trying to be their best.

Still, there's something about inviting someone to your place even if we aren't stripping off our clothes.

I open the door and wave an arm with a big flourish. "Welcome to my home."

Luke blows out a long, low whistle. "Wow. This is gorgeous!"

"Thanks. I like it too." I stand in the doorway and watch, fidgeting, as he walks around the living room. "At least the cave I live in is pretty."

"A cave? This is what you call a cave? Shit, I'd work from home all the time if I lived here."

I really am fortunate, and just about every guy I've dated has reminded me of that. I'm a lucky girl, and I know it. But, sometimes, it's awkward when they make a big deal about it.

The sound of a door opening behind me chills my blood. Darn it, I should've shut the door. I should've gone inside and shut the door and maybe installed soundproofing foam over the walls earlier today.

"Hey! I thought I heard you over here!" Matt doesn't even bother excusing himself before sliding past me and heading straight up to Luke, where they do their bro-hug thing.

"Is your apartment anything like this one?" Luke asks him, looking around again.

"Yeah but in a slightly more masculine color." Matt slides a look my way from the corner of his eye. "But otherwise, the layout is basically the same."

"Damn, I should've gotten into your line of work then."

Matt offers a wry chuckle. "Still teaching hockey clinics?"

"I've moved into more of a one-on-one training business."

I might as well not be here at all. It's like they've both completely forgotten I exist.

Matt turns to me. Either he heard my thoughts or felt the heat of my stare against the back of his head. "Sorry, I was rude to barge in like that."

I plaster on a sickly-sweet smile. "Oh, do you think so?"

He elbows Luke. "We sort of wander in and out of each other's apartments sometimes. Don't worry; I don't make a habit of it."

Luke laughs. "I was gonna say, you're making

me wonder if I have some competition."

Before Matt has a chance to say something obnoxious, I jump in. "You have no competition, Luke, just like how it is on the ice."

Bingo.

Matt goes stiff for a second but recovers quickly. "I was just about to put on a football game over at my place. Just got a new TV, and the picture is so clear, you would swear the players were right there in the room with you."

I see where this is going, and I'm about ready to scream.

Luke's brows lift. "No kidding? Can I come over and take a look?"

Damn him. If I argue, it'll look like I'm being childish, won't it? And it isn't like we were coming back here for the express purpose of taking our clothes off … though honestly, I was hoping to at least make out for a while.

Matt turns to me with a gleam in his eye I've seen way too many times to count. He knows exactly what he's doing, the jerk—though I have to wonder why. *What does he hope to gain by this?*

"That okay with you? I'm sure there were other things you were hoping to do tonight …"

"He's only going over to take a look, right? Besides"—I give Luke my most flirtatious smile—"you didn't give me the time to chain him to the radiator and keep him all to myself. Next time, I'll be quicker."

"I don't hate the sound of that." Luke kisses my cheek in passing. "Be right back."

Matt's behind him, and the relief of not having to keep a happy, pleasant expression anymore is palpable. There's no chance of him misunderstanding the utter disgust I'm feeling right now when it comes through in the way I scowl at him, turning away before he can say anything that I'm sure would only twist the knife.

What is his deal? Why is he acting like this? I want to ask him right now regardless of whether it makes me look petty and childish in front of Luke. Luke doesn't know our history—heck, half the time, I'm not even sure of our history. I certainly didn't expect Matt to kiss me. How many signs have I missed?

Instead of storming over there, which I really want to do, I settle for texting Hayley. *You're not going to believe this. Matt totally just cockblocked me.*

Hayley sends back a string of emojis, all with surprised faces. *You don't usually talk like that! What did he do?*

Luke's over there with him right now, checking out his brand-new TV with a football game on, instead of being over here with me.

Rather than texting back, she calls. "That dick! He invited Luke over?" She's practically screeching, which makes me feel a lot better. Like I'm not overthinking this.

"Yeah. Flat-out came over when he heard his voice and asked if he wanted to check out the TV. I mean, it's an amazing TV, don't get me wrong, but still."

"This is definite cockblockage. I mean, I've wanted to give him the benefit of the doubt up until now, but there's no way to misconstrue what he did. The man went out of his way to wedge himself between you two. That's not cool."

"No, it isn't."

"What are you going to do about it?"

"I don't know." I chew my thumbnail, staring at my open door. The door to Matt's place is open, too, giving me a look inside. "Son of a bitch, they're sitting down on the sofa."

"Wow. You don't usually break out the profanity. That's much more my department."

"This is a unique situation. Focus, please. I have no idea how to navigate this."

I hear murmuring in the background. Male murmuring. Immediately, I smack my palm to my forehead. "You're busy with Nicholas. I'm sorry."

"No, no. We're just hanging out, but hold on a minute."

I hear more murmurs and giggles. *Who is this woman? My happy best friend—that's who.*

I'm still fuming when I see Luke relax back into the sofa.

"Kitty, are you there?"

"Yes," I huff.

"Nicholas thinks Luke is out of his mind if he's watching football instead of being with you."

"I think I like this guy. You know I'll have to meet him soon."

"Sure, sure. So, what are you going to do?"

"I'm going to go give that cockblocker a piece of my mind."

"Go, Kitty. Meow," Hayley cheers before hanging up the phone with a giggle.

I rap on Matt's open door and stride in before closing it behind me. Both guys look up in surprise.

Oh, they thought I'd just sit idle while they watched the game. How cute.

"Matt, could I have a quick word with you?"

"Uh, sure." He looks to Luke like a child who's about to get into trouble.

He has no idea.

"What's up?" he asks once we get in the kitchen, out of earshot of Luke.

"*What's up?* What's up? For starters, you just barged into my home, uninvited, and then kidnapped my date, and now, you're watching a football game together. What the actual hell, Matt?"

"I just wanted to show him my new TV. I had no idea he'd stay."

"And you didn't think to send him back over?"

"No. I thought that would be rude. He's my friend."

"Huh, a friend who you wanted me to meet so I could date a hockey player for my book. So, what's with the cockblock?"

"Cockblock? Already? That's pretty fast for

you."

I throw my hands up in frustration. "That's not what I meant. I just meant that we were supposed to be getting to know one another, and you brought him over here. So, I ask again, what the hell?"

"Kitty, I'm sorry. I wasn't thinking. I haven't seen Luke in a while."

"Well, if you would so kindly help get him back over to my place, I would appreciate it."

"You could always join us and watch the game," Matt adds in a hopeful voice.

This is not at all how I saw this evening going, but I refuse to let Luke see me upset.

"Fine. You win," I growl.

"Great."

Matt strolls out of his kitchen with a carefree attitude while I shoot daggers out of my eyes at the back of his head. Men are so frustrating.

I follow him back into the living room, and I settle in next to Luke.

"Kitty's decided to watch the game with us. Is that cool with you, bro?" Matt asks Luke.

"Yeah, that would be great. Now, I can spend time with both of you."

"Let me grab you a beer. Kitty, do you want anything?"

I'm not sure Matt has enough alcohol to get me through the rest of the night, but I take a beer as well. While he gets them from the fridge, I pull my feet up on the couch and curl up next to Luke. If

Matt wants to play dirty, I can play dirty too.

For the rest of the game, we drink and talk. Actually, I drink, and they talk about hockey and football. I'm surprised they can even follow the game. At least I can follow football because I used to watch it with my dad when I was younger.

I also try to make sure Luke knows I'm here by rubbing his neck and gently stroking his arm and hand. At some point, he wraps his arm around my shoulders, and now, my head is resting on his chest. He's so warm and comfortable; I almost fall asleep until I'm startled awake when their team wins on the last play of the game. I yawn and sit upright.

"Wow, it's late. I need to get going, so I can practice in the morning. Thanks for the beers, Matt. That TV is amazing. I felt like we were watching from the sideline."

"It was awesome, man. I'm glad you could come over. It's been so long."

Luke stands and pulls me off the couch. "May I walk you home?" he asks with a grin.

"I'd hate for you to go out of your way," I say with a giggle.

"It's no trouble at all."

"Good night, Matt," I say over my shoulder, giving him a wink.

"Night, Kitty. Night, Luke."

Luke opens my door and pulls me into my apartment and into a big hug.

"Thanks for being such a good sport tonight. I

really didn't plan to stay over there. I really do want to get to know you, Kitty."

"I want to get to know you too. So, you think maybe next time, it could just be you and me? Sitting on my couch?" I ask.

"Definitely. Hey, can I ask you a question?"

"Sure."

"Do you think Matt's lonely?"

"Lonely? I don't think so. Why?"

"Just a feeling I get."

"Well, you aren't his neighbor, and I can assure you that Matt is not lonely. There are plenty of women coming and going out of that apartment."

"That's funny. He said he hasn't really been with anyone for a while."

"When did he tell you that?"

"I asked him if he was seeing anyone the other night, and he said no one worthwhile."

"Hmm, interesting. I didn't think guys talked about stuff like that."

"Yeah, well, sometimes, we do, and I thought it might be nice if I took him out this week. Maybe help him find someone."

"Oh yeah? Well, that's very sweet of you."

I give him a hug, and then he pulls me back in for a chaste kiss on the lips.

"I'd better go. I need to get some sleep. Good night, Kitty."

"Good night, Luke."

As I close the door behind him, I'm suddenly

annoyed. And I'm not sure it's because Luke is choosing to go out with Matt instead of me or if it's because they are going out to find Matt a new girlfriend.

Chapter Eleven

"SO, YOU HAVEN'T slept with him yet?"

I've been on the phone with my editor for all of three minutes, and she's already giving me a headache.

"No, we've only gone on a few dates, and on the last one, Matt invited him over to watch a game."

"Oh, Matt blocked you? Interesting. Very interesting. So, do you think the next book will be *Kitty Dates her Hot Neighbor?*"

"Maggie, just stop right there. I've already had to explain this to everyone else. Matt and I will never get together. We have nothing in common, and he's my neighbor."

"So?"

"So, I really like my apartment, and I don't want to have to move when it doesn't work out. You won't let me use my imagination anymore, so I can't stay with my neighbor forever if I'm writing these books."

"Hmm, point taken. Good thing we have lots of other tropes for you. Now, let's get this hockey book started. You've had plenty of time off, and while I've been doing some publishing magic, we need something new to keep you relevant. Things have changed so quickly. Readers are voracious in a way they never were before because, now, they feel they have all the content in the world at their fingertips. And for the most part, they do. But there's no satisfying them."

"I'm on it, Maggie."

"And, Kitty?"

Please don't say it. Please don't say it.

"Yes?"

"Don't forget to bring the heat."

"Haven't I proven myself by now?"

"Yes, but it never hurts to give us more. You know, character development is a thing in real life too."

"Right. Good-bye, Maggie."

"Bye, Kitty."

Now, all I have to do is write an absolutely sultry book. Just as my love life has been reduced to a simmer. No biggie. I can do this. Just wait until Maggie finds out I actually used my imagination for this one.

My hero and heroine—a hockey player and the sports writer working her fingers to the bone to be taken seriously in what's typically a male-dominated field—are currently in the locker room.

"How many women usually come in here?" She ran a hand over one of the tables, where she imagined players must sit after a tough game and allow the trainers to

stretch their sore muscles.

"Counting you? One that I've ever seen."

"Just one." It made her shiver, like she was an explorer in a new world. A pioneer.

"Yeah, even the lady reporters stay out of here. There aren't many of them that I know about though." He turned to her, leaning against the wall separating one locker from another. "We might have to cover up if a girl ever came in here, and there are some of us who don't like covering up."

"So, you just walk around, swinging free?"

"Why not? Might as well." When she made a face, he laughed. "It's not weird. By the time you make the pros, you've grown up in locker rooms. You've been around other guys your entire life. Undressing, showering, dressing. It's as natural as breathing. But you also get set in your ways, I guess. When you're not used to covering up because you didn't have to worry about it for twenty years …"

"I get it." She arched an eyebrow, her eyes flicking up and down over his impressive body. Even in a sweater and jeans, he was droolworthy. "Maybe I could dress up like a guy and sneak in here sometime. Sounds like there could be a lot of eye candy strutting around."

"Hey. There's only one piece of eye candy you should be interested in."

Her body flushed all over, her skin tingling. Even her nipples hardened under his gaze and the heaviness in his voice. There was now the promise of a lot more than the professional relationship they were currently in.

Now, it was like all the lines had been blurred. The

lines between what she needed from him—stories, legitimacy as a reporter—and what he needed from her.

What did he need from her? He had been doing fine on his own before she came along, before her editor put them together for a series. It wasn't like he needed his profile raised. If anything, his growing fame had started to pull focus from the rest of the team and ruffle some proud, egocentric feathers.

When she looked back at him, he was staring at her with his mouth twitching upward. He was smirking. He knew what he was doing to her, the way he made her feel, the thoughts he stirred up.

And he liked it.

He stalked across the room. Keeping eye contact. Ready to pounce.

She didn't look away, and she didn't back away and run for the door either. Her knees were shaking, and her heart was racing, but she refused to run.

She wanted this. She wanted him.

By the time the door opens behind me, the hero is on his knees, giving my heroine the most exquisite oral pleasure she's ever received.

Which, of course, is why Matt chooses this exact moment to walk in.

Why didn't I lock the damn door?

It takes a second for me to come back to reality; I was so wrapped up in my work and what was turning out to be a very steamy scene.

"Don't you ever knock? And now, you're interrupting my work. I was finally in a groove with this damn book, and you come strolling in."

All that, and I haven't even turned around yet.

"Wow. Anything else you want to accuse me of? Just get it all out of the way now. There was a cab stolen around the corner earlier this morning. Maybe I did that too."

I spin in my chair, and if there isn't fire flashing in my eyes—literal flames—I'd be surprised. He even takes a step back when he sees me.

"Okay, okay. I was a dick last night. I thought I'd buy you lunch to make up for it."

"Lunch? You think sesame tofu and an egg roll are going to make up for what you did last night? And you're admitting you were a dick too! The nerve!"

"You know what? I didn't come over here to be yelled at." He holds up his hands, surrendering. "I was trying to make it up to you."

"You can't just make it up to me. This isn't right, none of it."

"What does that mean? What are you talking about?" Now, his arms are folded, which I know means he's on the defensive. He's ready for war.

"You deliberately got in the way last night. You admitted it, and you admitted you were a dick about it. Why would you do that? Why help me meet Luke and then stand in the way of me spending time with him? What game are you playing?"

"Who said I'm playing a game? I don't have time for that."

"Bull. You're lying." I stand, facing him. "It's one thing for us to joke around and get on each other's nerves, but you have never deliberately stood in my way before. You've never sabotaged me."

"Valentine, you're letting your imagination—"

"Don't talk down to me." My voice is a hiss, sharp and dangerous, even to my own ears. "You're in my apartment right now, and you didn't even bother knocking. You walk in here like you own the place; you play games with my work!"

He rolls his eyes.

"Yes, my work!" I insist.

He clearly does not feel the same. "He's a person. A good guy. He's not your work. None of these guys you've dated are work. They're people. And you … you …"

"Use them? Is that what you're trying to say? I use people? Because let me tell you, you're not saying anything I haven't already thought before. But you know what else? I go into these new books and new relationships openly. With hope. Maybe it'll work out this time. Maybe this is the right person. And isn't that how normal relationships work?"

He snorts. "I haven't been in a relationship in a long time, so I couldn't tell you for sure."

Oh, man.

I shouldn't say it.

I should not.

I absolutely, a hundred percent need to bite my tongue to stop myself from saying something I will never be able to take back.

But dang it all, I want to. It'll feel so good to let him know what I know. To throw it in his face and watch him react. He's not the only one who can sling a barb.

I won't let him get away with thinking he has the upper hand.

Which is why I open my big, stupid mouth and let it pour out. "No, I guess it's been a while since your breakup with Ginger."

Bull's-eye.

I've never seen him go pale. His complexion is usually tan year-round, thanks to all the time he spends outside running, walking the dog.

Yet here he is, looking pale indeed. His eyes are wider than normal, too, and there's a flatness to them.

"Too far." He unfolds his arms, letting them fall to his sides. "You went too far."

I know it, and I already feel sorry. But I'm not about to agree with him. I mean, he deserved it.

"You went there first. I only followed you."

Now, his face is red, and I can't say I like that color much better. "Too far." That's all he manages to grunt before leaving, slamming the door hard enough to make the frame rattle.

Terrific. I'm officially a terrible person.

Chapter Twelve

IT'S BEEN A while since I've worked through the night. It's been a while since I've had a reason to.

Either I work until my eyes can't stay open any longer or I sit around, stewing over Matt and how disappointed I am in myself for sinking to his level.

Because after giving it some thought, it became clear, that was the real problem. Not what he said. Not what he did yesterday.

It was that I sank to his level. For some reason, he was being mean and rude, and I had to one-up him.

I succeeded. But I went too far. Lord knows he said it enough.

Did things end that badly with him and Ginger?

It's past three in the morning, and my eyes are starting to tire out when I hear footfalls in the hall. And stumbling. And drunken laughter.

And a girl's voice.

When there's a knock at my door, I cringe and then freeze that way. The lights are on, so I know they can see the glow under the door.

Who would knock at this time of night? I made it a

point to lock the door after Matt stormed out, just in case he was of a mind to storm back in. I'll be smarter about locking up from now on.

"Maybe she fell asleep on her computer," Matt slurs, but there's an edge in his voice, though what I hear a lot more clearly is the laughter of the girl. Whoever she is.

"Shh. Go on, do your thing," I hear Luke's voice say.

Another knock. So, they're finally home from carousing. At least he sounds soberer than Matt, who, come to think of it, I've never heard like this. He drinks but rarely gets drunk—that I'm aware of. He's always struck me as somebody in control of himself.

I tiptoe over to the door, holding my breath. Listening hard so I can hear when the door to Matt's apartment closes. I can't see him right now. I don't even want to set eyes on him.

As soon as I hear the click of his lock, I unlock my door and open it a crack.

Luke's standing there with a grin. "Hey. He told me you might be awake."

"Oh, did he?" I shoot a glare at the closed door across from mine. "That was nice of him."

"Sorry." He offers a sheepish look with a shrug. "I can go. I just figured if you were up ..."

I look him up and down, opening the door wider now. "You figured you'd come by and ask for the tour I wasn't able to give you yesterday? Or you just wanted to tuck me in for the night?"

"Something like that."

"Come on in then."

I close the door behind him but not before a burst of raucous laughter from across the hall sets my teeth on edge. Whoever she is, she's having a good time.

"Mind if I have some water? I never drink much, but still, I like to stay hydrated." He points to the kitchen, and I nod in encouragement.

"You were a good boy tonight then?"

"Sure. I usually am. I can't abuse my body that way. A beer or two—that's it."

"I admire you. You're so focused on your goals." I lean against the island and admire other things about him that have nothing to do with goals. Though really, I guess they do since his fitness is directly tied to how well he performs on the ice.

Another burst of laughter from Matt's. Even Luke hears this. "Is it always so easy to hear what goes on over there?"

"You have no idea." I roll my eyes with a groan. "For a long time, before we ever officially met, the most I knew about him was how he made girls scream his name."

"Wow. Good for him. Not so good for you."

"No, it wasn't a lot of fun, especially since I tend to work late at night."

He finishes off the water and tosses the bottle

into the recycling bin before coming to me. "You talk about admiring me, and you're working at three in the morning."

"It's usually when I do my best writing."

He stands roughly an inch from me, so close that I can feel the heat of his breath on my face. "What else can you tell me? I want to know all about you."

"Hmm. I practice yoga."

"You do, huh? I wondered how you kept in such good shape."

"Not nearly as good as you." I take a chance and trace his bicep with one fingertip. It's impressive. Extremely. "But it does help me stay flexible."

A devilish grin. "How does that help a writer?"

"It doesn't. But it helps at other times—when I'm not writing."

"Oh?" He lowers his head slowly, inch by inch. "Like when?"

It's not easy, finding the breath to respond. "Like when a hockey player shows up at my door at three in the morning, looking and smelling so good that I don't know if I can handle myself."

"Do me a favor." His lips are almost touching mine, and, oh, my heart is pounding hard enough to drown out every sound but his voice. "Don't try too hard."

Then, he sweeps me up in a kiss, arms tight around me, holding me close. I wrap my arms around his neck and let him pick me up and carry me to the bedroom.

So, this is happening. This is really happening.

And I want it. I need it.

"Oh … oh yeah … oh yeah, baby …"

I can't believe this. This can't be happening. Luke doesn't seem to notice, too busy pulling off his shirt and unbuttoning his jeans. I should be focused on him. I want to be focused on him. He's freaking glorious. He's standing next to the bed and ready to pounce on me, and all I can hear is some random girl getting off on the other side of the wall.

Luke kisses me, kisses my neck, while his hands run over me. Yes, this is what matters; this is where I am. Here, in this moment, with this man in my bed. The pressure against my thigh reminds me of just how much he wants to be here, too, with every thrust of his hips against me as he lowers my shorts.

"Matt! Oh, fuck, yes!"

Okay, I know he heard that.

Luke jerks, surprised. "Are you serious?" It's a low murmur against my chest, where he was just putting his lips.

"Don't pay attention." I take his face in my hands and pull him in for a kiss while Miss Whatever Her Name Is screams like the world's crashing down around her.

But I can tell it's distracting, the screaming and moaning. He lifts his head, glancing at the wall.

Then he looks down at me with a gleam in his eye. "Wanna see if we can do better?"

Oh, yes, I do.

And by the time we're finished, I'm hoarse and sweaty and exhausted.

"I think … we won," I manage to pant out between breaths.

"I knew we would." He gets up and comes back with two bottles of water, one of which I gratefully accept.

"I'm sorry for what was going on next door. It was—"

"Don't even mention it. Hey, I'm glad he got laid. Though he didn't have to try too hard. That's one area he's never had trouble with."

No, he sure doesn't.

Luke sits up against the headboard, a sheet over his lap. I could spend hours doing nothing but staring at him, that body, those hands. Maybe I'm not so tired of writing for tropes.

"I still think it's obnoxious," I have to admit. "He's mad at me right now, so I'm sure that had something to do with it. But it's been a long time since he brought a random girl home. Imagine having to hear that three or four nights a week."

"You have to cut him some slack. I know he's a pain in the ass, but …" He scrubs his fingers through his hair until it stands on end, glowing in the light from my nightstand lamp. "It's not for me to talk about."

I turn on my side, propping myself up on one elbow. "Ginger?"

"You know?"

"Partially. I haven't talked about it with him."

"I didn't think you had. He would never want to bring it up. It was a bad time. So bad that he quit the team."

My throat tightens. Damn it, I didn't want to go into this, and I sure don't want to feel sorry for him. The jerk.

Even so, now that the door's open, I can't help but go through it.

"Can I guess what happened?"

He nods.

"Ginger broke it off with him and started dating Mark."

"Basically, yeah. The three of us were all on the same team. It was fun, you know? But Matt didn't want to go pro. He liked playing in college, but it wasn't his long-term goal, like it was for me and Mark. He and Ginger were dating and getting serious, but once she found out he had other career plans, well …"

"She dropped Matt and hooked up with Mark?" I finish for him.

"She wants to be a pro athlete's wife. He was head over heels in love, and I guess she didn't feel the same way." He turns to me with a snicker. "We're talking about other people right now. What's wrong with us?"

I have to laugh too. "You'd think, since I'm a romance author, my pillow-talk game would be on point."

"You write perfect situations though, I bet." He flops back down next to me, tucking a strand of hair behind my ear and cupping my cheek when he's finished. "Your characters don't have to suffer through people having obnoxiously loud sex with a thin wall between apartments."

"That could be a funny twist." I lean in to kiss him, silently deciding to focus only on him now. "I think we did a good job of drowning them out though."

His brows lift. "Wanna go for round two?"

I wind an arm around his neck, pulling him down on top of me. "I thought you'd never ask."

Chapter Thirteen

"My first game. This is so exciting!" I cheer as I sit down next to Darcy, who's becoming a good friend.

Not only does she give me the behind-the-scenes scoop of being a hockey girlfriend, but she's also a nice person with a good heart.

Thank goodness I have her. I mean, who else could I rely on? Ginger? No, thank you. I'm too weirded out by her having dated Matt and, evidently, breaking his heart in a big way.

Darn it. I have to stop thinking about him. When did he start entering my thoughts at random times like this? And why, especially when he's not my favorite person right now?

"It's so weird, seeing the rink full like this."

There isn't an empty seat anywhere, which, for some reason, fills me with a sense of pride. All these people came out to watch Luke play.

Okay, not only him, but still. They won't be able to take their eyes off him; I'm sure of it. And I sort of wish I had a jersey with his number on it, just so everybody knew …

What? That we're sleeping together? Get real, Valen-

tine. He hasn't promised you anything. Right. Just because he's good in bed—no, insatiable—doesn't mean I'm jersey-worthy yet.

I have to keep my heart out of this.

Maybe somebody should remind said heart of that since it skips a beat when Luke sails onto the ice with the rest of the team. I clap until my hands hurt and shout until I'm almost as hoarse as I was after that first time the other night. And the second.

He looks great out there. I make a mental note to describe the absolute thrill of watching him glide effortlessly across the ice with determination and focus. He works hard. He deserves the screams from the fans when his name is announced over the sound system.

Once the game begins, I don't know where to look. The practices I observed were fast-paced but nothing compared to an actual game. "I can't keep up!"

"You get used to it," Darcy assures me without taking her eyes off the players.

"How long does it take?"

"It takes a while. But I was already into hockey when I—"

Suddenly, Luke scores, and we leap to our feet, screaming.

"I didn't even see him get the puck!"

"That's how he is. It's practically impossible to catch him!" Darcy's eyes shine, and I can only imagine mine do too.

My heart's pounding a mile a minute when we sit down. Just like that, the action on the ice gets going again with players crisscrossing and passing the puck back and forth. I glance over at the net and wonder what it must be like for the goalie, knowing so much is on his shoulders.

Me? I'd cross my arms over my head and curl up in a ball. I wouldn't want a two-hundred-pound hockey player in full pads and sharp skates crashing into me. And I sure wouldn't want our team's fate in my hands. Talk about anxiety.

I practically jump out of my skin when one of the other team's players slams one of our players into the wall not far away from where I'm sitting. It's bone-jarring. "How do they manage to make it through that?"

It's a rhetorical question. But dang, I don't know if I'd be able to keep skating and playing like nothing happened after getting slammed into like that.

No wonder fights break out. I'd be raring for a fight too.

By the end of the first period, we're up a single point. Luke's goal. Our goalie is so fast, so agile, it seems that nothing can get past him.

That changes in the second period when they score two goals on him. I can feel the energy lagging, even among the girlfriends and wives surrounding me. Ginger tries to rally everybody, to get us to chant in unison, but even that's not enough to overcome the roar from the opposing team's fans as they cheer their second goal.

"It's a lot more fun when we're on top, isn't it?" I muse to Darcy, who can only sigh.

"You get used to this too," she explains. "They can't win every game. But there's a third period to go. Anything could happen."

But here's the thing I'm learning as the clock ticks down toward the end of the game and our team is down one goal: it's not easy to have a cool head and play evenly, skillfully when time is running out.

"Ouch!" I grimace in horror when one of the other team's players crashes into the wall, followed by none other than Mark. "Did he need to hit him that hard?"

Darcy's either unable or unwilling to answer. Probably too wrapped up in what's going on in front of us—or maybe she's tired of hearing my questions. Besides, there's no way to answer. We're not the ones playing the game, so we can't really judge what's going on down there.

Suddenly, there's loud shouting from the other side of the ice. The people sitting behind the Plexiglass push on the barrier when two players begin throwing fists.

And, oh my God, one of them is Luke.

"No, no!" I try to keep my feelings to myself since this is their world, not mine.

The people around me know more about the

game than I do, and they don't seem as upset about this as I am.

Well, they're not the one dating one of the players currently ripping off his helmet throwing punch after punch with one hand while holding the guy's jersey in the other, keeping him in place.

And the people sitting just behind them? They're loving it, screaming for blood, practically salivating. It's primal, violent; they're thirsty for it. I don't think I've ever seen football fans act this way. They scream and shout and whatnot, but they don't actively cheer like they want to see somebody's head pop off and slide across the field.

Needless to say, both Luke and the player he fought end up in the penalty box. I can't hear Luke's shouting—but I don't need to. I can read his lips and his face, and I know exactly what's he saying.

"Does he do a lot of that?" I ask. After the way he reacted to that drunk guy at dinner, I have to know what I'm getting into.

"Hmm?" She glances my way. "Does he? Oh, no more than anybody else." Then, she touches my arm, frowning. "Are you worried about that? Because you don't have to be. Just because they're violent out there doesn't mean they're violent anywhere else. If anything, playing hard and fighting helps work all that stuff out of their system."

I can understand that. I don't have to love it, but I understand it. I would feel the same way if he played any sport.

Although I don't think fistfights are common in golf.

It's killing Luke to be penalized. I can just tell. He wants to be out on the ice, helping his team win. Or at least helping them tie things up. He's like a caged tiger, vibrating with energy, banging the end of his hockey stick against the floor as he shouts to the players on the ice.

The clock's ticking, ticking, and it doesn't look like we have a chance in hell of winning—until Mike scores and we have a reason to stand up and cheer again. He's not the fastest or best player, but he's good at feinting in one direction and shooting in another.

Luke comes flying out of the penalty box the very second he can, and the most amazing thing I've witnessed tonight by far is how the energy on the ice changes when he's out there. He's like lightning, zipping and zapping this way and that, and he forces the other players on both teams to elevate their game when he's around.

He's an inspiration. He's a magnet, drawing my gaze. I follow him, follow his movements, his smooth skating. God, it's like he's in an entirely different league.

And he wants to be. Honestly—and not just because we're dating—I think he deserves to be. He deserves to have his endlessly hard work pay off.

And when he scores the winning goal with only

fifteen seconds left on the clock, the roof almost blows off. I don't think I've ever screamed so loud in my life.

He looks so happy. Like he's where he belongs.

Darcy throws her arms around me. "I'm so glad you were here for that!" she screams, and we both jump up and down.

I'm glad too. I'm glad I got to see him win the game for his team. It's like he had to get that last hit in against his opponent after the fight on the ice earlier.

And he did. Is it wrong that I'm thrilled he did?

By the time it's all over, I'm wiped out. "God, how do you manage to go through that game after game? I don't think my heart could've handled much more."

"It's exciting, isn't it?" Her eyes shine, and her face is flushed. "It's like foreplay."

"Darcy!" But I can't help laughing because she's right. I'm excited all over.

And judging from Luke's affectionate greeting when he finds me outside the locker room, I'm not alone in this. "Come on. I don't feel like going out with the team tonight."

"You're sure about that?" I mean, it's not like I don't want him to take me home and ravish me, but still. "I don't want to get in the way of you and the team. They'll give you hell for letting me lure you away, and you know it."

"That's what I like most about you, I think." He

kisses me again and lets his hands roam more than I'm comfortable with in public.

"What's that?" I manage to pull his hands up from my butt until they're resting at my waist.

"You're so unselfish. You actually care about what the team thinks. You don't want to make my life complicated."

"Isn't that how it's supposed to be?"

"I always suspected, but that's not how it's been with other girls I've dated." He casts a look over his shoulder, where more of the team is now leaving the locker room in search of some postgame fun. "Okay, one beer. Then, we'll work on breaking that bed of yours."

I never would've imagined the thought of a broken bed sending a happy shiver up my spine. But I wouldn't have imagined getting turned on by a hockey game either. It's that sort of night, I guess.

Chapter Fourteen

"WHAT DO YOU think?"

What do I think? I think this is a mistake. I think I hate feeling like a dress-up doll.

But since this is all in service of my grandmother's big day, I need to bite my tongue rather than complain.

She's behind me, seated on a sofa, enjoying a glass of champagne offered by the salesclerk. I can see her in the mirror, watching. Trying to look like she doesn't have an opinion when I know for a fact that the woman's never been without an opinion in her entire life.

She doesn't want to sway my feelings.

Well, she couldn't possibly make me dislike this entire situation more. I don't like having to look at myself in a three-way mirror, having strangers commenting on my less than perfect figure.

I'm in a pink dress, though it's a subtle pink with an almost-gray undertone. It's satin, and it's not exactly forgiving, snug at the hip, all the way down to my knees. "This isn't exactly my style." That's diplomatic at least. I'm proud of myself for being so dignified in my response.

"This isn't about your style, Kathryn."

"I know. It's about your wedding."

"And having you beside me."

She's right. I stand up straighter. The woman wants me to be her maid of honor, for heaven's sake. I cried buckets when she asked.

Even now, afraid to move too much, for fear of being impaled by a pin, I could burst out crying. My grandmother's not much for emotional gestures, but she knows how to hit me in the heart when she feels like it.

"If you like it, I like it." I smile at her in the mirror, and it's a real smile, not something faked for her sake. "It'll look great next to your cream suit too."

"Many dresses will look fine beside my suit, dear, though having you in one will elevate it quite a bit. What use would it be if I placed a clothing rack next to me?"

She stands, folding her arms with a critical expression. "They cinched it too tight about the waist and at the bust. You have a lovely figure, but no woman feels confident when she's stuffed into a sausage casing. May I?" She's already handing over her champagne flute before she steps up behind me and starts releasing the pins holding the dress so close to my body.

The girl's face is slack, pale, but she can only stand back and watch.

Grandmother must realize the effect she's having on the clerk. She chuckles. "When you've been through as many fittings as I have in my seventy-six years, you have no choice but to learn what's what. I would never consider myself a professional, but I've had my figure commented upon more times than I could hope to count. Which I most decidedly do not."

The girl meets my eyes in the mirror.

"Yeah, try growing up with her as a grandmother."

Grandmother scoffs, busy with her work, "One should be so lucky."

She's not wrong. And she's not wrong about her skills as a dress fitter either because by the time she's finished adjusting the dress, it fits like it was meant for me. I can actually move without being afraid I'll split a seam.

"See?" Grandmother strolls around in front of me, nodding slowly. "She looked like a dominatrix before, as if it had been painted on her. All she was missing was a pointed bra."

"Oh my God." I'm dying for this poor girl, whose face went from milky to blood red in the blink of an eye.

"Well, you did. Wearing something so tight. Can you imagine? And to a wedding."

I catch the girl's eye. *I'm sorry*, I mouth.

Any more of this, and she'll end up quitting her job. I wouldn't blame her if she had any other clients like my grandmother.

When we're relatively alone—the clerk scurried away with the champagne flute, maybe intending to down the rest of the bottle—I scowl at Grandmother. "You were mean. She was only doing her best."

"She was doing you a disservice." She straightens the hem along the bottom of the dress, which no longer hugs my knees but rather skims them. "If she wants to keep her job, she'd better improve at it. I could just as easily complain to her supervisor, but I won't. How many people do you believe would be so generous as to offer free advice?"

Boy, she has a way of turning things around, so she sounds like the heroine, doesn't she? I wish I were half as smooth as she is. And half as sure of myself.

"Well, I think this is the winner." I turn to face her, arms out to my sides. "What's the verdict?"

"I think it goes beautifully with your coloring and will look divine beside my cream suit." She winks, eyes sparkling. "It isn't fair for the maid of honor to outshine the bride, but I knew what I was getting into when I asked you to stand up with me."

"Oh, please. You turn heads everywhere you go."

That's not just lip service either. She's not only beautiful. She has a regal quality too. Class, effortless grace, refinement.

Even if she has a bad habit of bringing up pointed bras and dominatrices in fancy boutiques that offer champagne and charcuterie to their patrons. And she's not one to stand back and explain what she thinks is the right thing, not when she has confidence in herself to get the job done. Why waste time suffering fools?

"Even so." She pats my arms with an approving smile. "Oh, to be your age again. No, actually, I take it back. I believe I enjoy this age much more. I know who I am. I know what I want out of life. And I know there isn't any time to sit back and wait for others to do things. If I want something done correctly, I must do it myself."

"I wish I had your confidence. I'm always worried I'll end up doing something the wrong way. Making a mistake."

"Mistakes." She waves a careless hand, giving me a scornful look. "Mistakes happen regardless. So long as you're breathing, my dear, you will make mistakes. Is that any reason to hold yourself in one place, saying and doing nothing?"

"I didn't say that."

"That is the only alternative to making mistakes though. That is the point I'm driving at. If you're alive and breathing, mistakes are bound to happen. But is there ever so grievous a mistake that we can't hope to recover?"

Is there? "I'm starting to wonder."

"What does that mean? What are you concerned about?"

"No, we don't have to talk about it now. Or

ever." I step down from the platform I've been standing on all this time. "I need to get out of this before I do something to ruin it before the wedding."

"Don't believe I'll forget what you said so easily. I might be an old woman, but I still possess all of my faculties."

Yes, she does. In fact, they seem to have gotten sharper with age.

It isn't until we sit down to lunch at The Plaza that she brings it up again. Here I am, trying to forget the fact that Paxton stayed here, that I spent more than one night here with him, and she's pestering me.

"So, what is it you've done that you don't believe can be undone?" She spreads a napkin over her lap before picking up her cup of tea.

"It's not such a big deal, really."

"Dear, if you brought it up from seemingly nowhere, it means something to you. Which makes it, as you put it, a big deal. Really."

The woman is impossible.

"You remember Matt."

"Who could forget him? You talk about him all the time. And he's tall with all that thick brown hair. And those eyes! Oh, he has the most marvelous eyes. And a body—"

"Yes, yes, fine, you know him." I swear, she's on a mission to embarrass me to death. "Anyway, we had a fight. A bad one. I feel terrible about it.

Though he started it, if that matters."

"It does, and it doesn't. I'm sure once you got started and the two of you began shouting things back and forth, it didn't matter much at all just who'd fired the first shot. It never does in the end."

She's right—at least, mostly. "He got in the way of a date I was on, and he admitted it to me. It was a deliberate act of sabotage."

"Sounds like something out of a Cold War spy movie."

"Come on."

She chuckles, lowering her cup. "Does it come as any surprise? This is the same Matt who carried me up six flights of stairs to be sure I was able to attend your rooftop birthday party. And I remember the kiss he laid on you."

"Sure, sure, but nothing ever came of that."

"Except for his blatant sabotage of a date you were on."

"I figured it had more to do with me being on a date with a friend of his."

Her eyebrows basically leave her forehead; she raises them so far. "You're dating a friend of his now? This hockey player?"

"He's the one who introduced us!" I sit back, shamefaced since I probably shouldn't be raising my voice in here. Certain things just aren't done.

In a near whisper, I explain, "Turns out, Matt used to play hockey. I thought it was convenient when he offered to introduce me to his friends. And it was. I only met Luke, thanks to him."

"I wonder if he regrets introducing you two now."

"Too bad."

She looks so disappointed that I want to crawl into a hole and stay there. It's not fair that she's such a pro at looking disappointed. The woman doesn't have to say a word. The way she screws her face up and tightens her mouth says it all.

"Kathryn, you must know how difficult it would be for someone who is fond of you to see you dating someone else."

"We're not dating though. We never have. If he feels that way about me, why hasn't he ever said anything?"

"Do you want to know what I suspect?"

"Please."

"He's kept his feelings to himself for the sake of your career."

Gulp.

That can't be true, can it?

Of course, this is the exact moment when our server brings a tray of sandwiches and places it on the table.

We both murmur our thanks before I lean in. "That's not true."

"How would you know?" She chooses a cucumber sandwich, eyeing me the whole time. "Has he ever told you so?"

"Of course not."

"Have you ever asked?"

"I'd rather eat my tongue."

"It doesn't appear your tongue has made it onto our sandwich tray."

"Well, there you go."

I can't believe she's snickering at this like it's funny. "Would you like to hear what a lifetime has taught me? Since we were only just talking about wisdom and experience, I see fit to share what I've learned."

"If you must."

"I must." She looks me dead in the eye, straight-faced. "Talk to him, for God's sake. Come out and speak to him about it. Ask him. What does he feel? What does it all mean?"

"If he would even talk to me after what I said to him."

"Something tells me I don't want to know about that."

"No, you probably don't."

"Talk to him anyway. He seems like a very fine young man—aside from his impressive physical qualities. Regardless of any romantic entanglements, I would hate to see you lose him as a friend. Communication is the cornerstone of any relationship, whether it be platonic or not."

"Do you and Peter have such open, honest communication?"

Her mouth twitches, though I can tell she's not completely amused. "I was unaware we would be dissecting my relationship."

"We aren't. Don't get so touchy."

"She tells me not to be touchy."

Now, she's smiling full-on, which is a relief.

"Yes, to answer your question. There are no uncertainties between us. I know where he stands; he knows where I stand. You know better than nearly anyone how appalling I find the idea of withholding my opinion."

"No comment."

"Which is in and of itself a comment."

Wow. Didn't I just have the same exchange with Hayley recently? It's funny, the way my tendencies reflect hers. I didn't mean to absorb so much of her, but I guess it's impossible not to once you've known someone long enough. And we are blood-related after all.

"So"—her voice is crisper, sharper, telling me the topic has shifted and right on time since I'm getting tired of hearing myself talk about my problems—"what do you think about the flowers? You know my preference for roses, but peonies and hydrangea have caught my fancy as of late."

Chapter Fifteen

"YOU'RE SURE THIS is a good idea?"

Luke looks up at me from where he's kneeling at my feet. Under any other circumstances, this would be a major turn-on. Who wouldn't want a man like him at their feet? Oh, the fantasies I could spin up out of this situation.

If the situation didn't include wearing ice skates.

"Why not? It's just us. I told you, hardly anybody ever comes out to skate this early in the morning."

Yes, and if it wasn't for him urging me to do this, I wouldn't be up this early to do nearly anything. How he does this every morning is a mystery to me.

"The things I do for research."

His laughter rings out in the big, empty space. "Research? Is that what I am to you?"

"You know you're more than that. But it takes a lot to get me on the ice. The last time I skated, I ended up with a sore butt for days."

"If your butt gets sore, I can always massage it for you."

"Ooh, I think it's feeling sore right now, come to think of it."

"Nope. You're not gonna get out of this." He pulls me to my feet and then helps me onto the ice. "Take your time. This isn't the same as navigating skaters at Rockefeller Center. It's just you and me."

"I can just as easily make a fool out of myself when no one else is around."

"Who cares about making a fool of yourself? I mean it." He takes my hands and skates backward, pulling me along with him. He's even graceful and sure-footed when skating in reverse.

"Nobody likes feeling foolish." Though right now, with him leading me, with our hands linked, it's easier to feel relaxed. He's got this under control.

"No, but you have to learn to get through it and move on. Like skating in a way." He smoothly leads me in a turn, so we don't hit the wall. Even with his back to it, it's like he sensed its nearness. I guess he's spent enough time in the rink to know it like the back of his hand.

"What do you mean?"

"So long as you keep moving, you're golden. If you hesitate or think too much about how your ass will ache if you fall, guess what happens?"

"Oh, I see."

"You have to have more faith in yourself. Even if you fall, you'll get back up. And there isn't a single person in the world who's ever laced up a pair of skates who hasn't landed on their ass. So, everybody can relate, and nobody will think twice about it."

"You think that applies to the rest of life too?"

What is he? Yoda or something? A guru?

"I do. Don't you? It's no good, getting too wrapped up in what might happen or what could go wrong. You waste the here and now when you're concerned with the future, even a few minutes from now."

That I can understand.

"Get out of your head and let your body do the thinking. You think too much anyway."

He then does maybe the worst possible thing.

He lets go of me.

"What are you doing? Where are you going?" It's a squeak. I basically sound like a rubber duck.

"Over here. Come on. Meet me at the other end." He glides backward, effortless, like he was born wearing skates.

I hate him right now.

What did he say about getting out of my head? I have to let my body do the thinking. That's good for him since my body likes him a lot more than my head does right now.

Okay, I can do this. I can glide like a swan over a lake. I can glide like I was born to do this. And if I fall? I fall.

And I do.

Down I go with a bone-jarring crash. "Ow …" I

want to bury myself someplace, especially since my butt is just about screaming and reminding me why this wasn't a good idea in the first place.

"Oh no!" He's laughing but gently as he skates back to me. "Okay, I didn't know you would fall that fast. You're not extremely coordinated, are you?"

"Gee, you'd think I would've warned you. Oh yeah, I did!" I reach up for him, and he helps me stand.

"Sorry. I didn't know it was possible for anybody to be so uncoordinated."

"I cannot stand you."

"You're right. I shouldn't laugh." He pulls me into a hug, which I also sort of wish he wouldn't do since now I have to make sure I don't fall and take him down with me. A lot of good it would do, injuring the star of the team.

"Come on. We'll take you to the locker room for some liniment."

I let him lead me from the ice since, as far as I'm concerned, I've spent enough time out here to last the rest of my life.

"Is it okay? Me going into the locker room?"

"Sure. Nobody else will be there. Only team members are allowed in the team locker room. I don't think anybody will mind if I bring a guest, just this once."

And that's how we end up alone in the locker room, which, surprisingly, isn't too far off from what I imagined for my book. It's colder, more sterile and bleaker, but otherwise, close to what I envisioned.

It's so hard not to think about work, even when I tell myself I have to live in the moment. *Wasn't that what Luke just warned me about?*

"I feel like I'm always in two places at once."

He helps me onto one of the tables. "What do you mean?"

I fold my arms under my head and rest my cheek against them with a sigh. "My head is always partially in my work. Wondering how to get past a sticky spot, how to transition from one beat to another without being too clunky or obvious. Transitions have always given me trouble. Whether I should polish something further, whether my descriptions are realistic enough ..."

"Got it." He slowly rubs my back in big circles. "I sort of know what you're talking about. All my decisions have to be about the game. Training. What'll help me, what'll hurt me."

His hands move over my sore thighs and butt, warming the muscles, even through my jeans.

"Maybe it was worth falling just for this."

"Hmm. I was thinking the same thing. Wondering why I didn't get you out on the ice sooner."

"Funny. You wouldn't feel the same way if your butt were so sore."

"Like I've never fallen. Like I've never had to spend nights sleeping on my stomach when being on my back was hell. Forget sitting. If I could've stood all day at school, I would have."

His thumbs, meanwhile, are now stroking my inner thighs.

"That part doesn't hurt," I murmur, though I don't exactly swat his hands away either. I'm not insane.

"Ever do it in a locker room?"

"What?" I barely have time to understand what he just asked before he flips me over onto my back. "Ouch!"

"Sorry. I'll make it feel better." He's already working on my button, my zipper.

"Luke! Here?"

"Nobody will come in. Trust me. It's been cleaned, and I'm the only home team member ever here at this time of the morning." He glances up at me with a wicked grin. "Though I guess we'd better get to it before someone does stroll in."

"Oh my God ..." I close my eyes and wonder what the heck is happening to me. Who am I turning into? One of the girls I write about?

Holy smokes, I already wrote a scene like this!

There I go again, thinking about work.

I have to be inside my body, not in my head. I especially want to be because the man knows what he's doing. Already, my jeans are off while he kisses his way up the insides of my legs until I shiver in anticipation.

One thing I know for sure as he works his magic

on me: there's truth to what people say about the threat of being discovered. It does make everything more exciting. I have to clench my fist and press it against my mouth to hold back the moans I know would attract attention from anybody who happened to be passing by.

He pulls me up to the very edge of the table and gets on his knees. Oh my God, he's very good at this. Better than anybody I've ever been with. It isn't long before I'm biting my knuckles and squeezing his head between my thighs, hoping like hell in the tiny corner of my brain that's processing thought that we aren't discovered just when I'm in the throes of passion.

But we aren't. Everything's quiet when Luke goes back to kissing the insides of my legs before moving on to other things.

When he raises his head, looking at me over the length of my torso, he asks the very last question I would ever expect to hear at a time like this, "Will you come to dinner with my family?"

Chapter Sixteen

"I'M NERVOUS."

"I can tell."

I turn in my seat to glare at Luke, who's smirking like the cat who might not have eaten the cream but who very much knows where the cream is kept and how to get at it. "Thanks. It would've been nicer if you'd told me there was nothing to be nervous about."

"I'm sure I've told you that. When I first asked you to come for dinner." He holds up one finger. "When you called me later to ask if I meant it when I asked you to come to dinner."

"Okay …"

A third finger. "This morning." A fourth. "Before we got in the car."

"I get it."

"I've told you again and again there's nothing to be worried about. My family is just a bunch of regular people. Dad's a teacher. Mom took time off work to raise the kids and then went back to school for social work. They've lived in the same row home for thirty years and just paid off the mortgage. You can't get more regular than them."

"They sound great, but what will they think of me?" And oh, dear Lord, why do I care so much? It's not like we're planning on getting married or even dating exclusively.

This is just another Sunday dinner with nice people who are generous and kind enough to allow me in their home.

But I do want them to like me. I want everybody to like me. Maybe too much.

"Do you think they'll like the flowers?" I'm holding a bouquet I painstakingly chose from the flower shop down the street. It took way more time than I feel comfortable with, but I wanted it to be perfect.

"They'll love them. And of course, Mom will say you didn't need to go to the trouble."

"It's rude to show up empty-handed. My grandmother would clutch her pearls and go into a tailspin if she ever suspected I'd considered not bringing something."

"Your grandmother sounds like she's a bit high society compared to my family. Like I said, they're just regular people."

I try not to stiffen at the way he makes it sound like being *regular* is better than whatever he thinks my grandmother is. And I don't love it. I don't care how much money you make. I care about what kind of person you are and how you treat others.

But then he redeems himself by squeezing my

knee and adding, "They'll like you just as much as I do. I promise."

The house he pulls in front of reminds me of where I grew up and it helps me relax a little.

He parks the car—a modest car that probably doesn't get a lot of use with him living in the city—and we head up to the front porch of a neat home tucked in the middle of a long line of almost-identical buildings. Only the ramp leading to the porch sets it apart from the rest of the houses.

And the second the door opens, it's like love explodes all around us.

"There he is!" A petite woman who shares Luke's coloring comes out from the kitchen, holding a wooden spoon. "I'm surprised I recognize you; it's been so long!"

"Mom, I was here three weeks ago." He hugs her with laughter in his voice. "You always say that."

"Just like I always remind you of the years I spent seeing you every single day. Not to mention, the time we shared a body. You can't expect a mother to adjust so easily."

She then turns to me with a beaming smile. "You must be Kitty. You're so beautiful."

I'm so charmed to the point of forgetting how to speak that I thrust the bouquet her way. "For you. Just a little something."

"Oh, they're gorgeous! You didn't have to do that!"

"Told you," Luke murmurs with a grin.

"Well, she didn't. You are very rude." She gives him a gentle elbow to the gut before turning back to me. "They really are gorgeous, but you didn't have to go to the trouble. I'm Luke's mother, as I'm sure you've already deduced."

"I have, Mrs. Costello."

"Please, call me Marie. I'd better get these into some water. Luke, help our guest make herself at home. Get her something to drink." She's out of the room, on her way to the kitchen, issuing orders.

Luke mimes a salute before blowing out a deep sigh. "So, there she is. My mom. I told you she wouldn't bite."

"She seems great. And like she doesn't take any crap from you, which is exactly how you need to be treated."

"Ouch." He pretends to be hurt, grimacing. "If I'd have known you'd gang up on me, I wouldn't have offered to bring you to dinner."

"Too late now." I spin in a slow circle, taking in the living room and dining room beyond that. "This is a nice house. Did you play a lot in the backyard?"

"Sure. But we spent more time out front, on each other's stoops and out in the street."

"Let me guess. You were playing hockey?"

He rolls his eyes. "I was playing whatever was being played. Stickball, kickball, even basketball. And, yeah, hockey every once in a while, but moving the nets every time a car came by got to be a pain in the ass."

"Language!"

I have to press my lips together tight to keep from laughing at Marie's sharp rebuke from the kitchen. She's completely out of sight and two rooms away, but somehow, she heard him. A mom's superpower.

"Sorry." He rubs a hand over the back of his neck. "I swear, I spend two minutes here, and I might as well be ten years old again."

The wall above the overstuffed sectional sofa is covered in framed photos. Most of them involve boys in sports equipment.

"Is this you or your brother?" I ask, pointing to one of a young boy with a gap-toothed smile, holding up a trophy almost as tall as he is.

"That's Liam. We were … eleven, I think, and our team won the state championship."

"Hockey?"

"What else?" He points to the figure on top of the trophy, which is very obviously a player holding a hockey stick.

"Duh," I mutter at myself, moving on to the next photo and the next.

It's not only pictures either. There are news clippings mixed in, stories praising the twin brothers who seemed to read each other's minds out on the ice.

"Did you really?"

"Did I what?" He stands behind me. I can see

him in the reflection from the glass.

"Read each other's minds on the ice?"

He turns his head away ever so slightly. "It wasn't conscious. But maybe we did. You know what they say about twins. It's a natural telepathy. Even now, sometimes, I get these feelings from out of nowhere. Like he's in a jam and he needs a few bucks. And there've been times when I was hurt or in a tight spot, and he'd suddenly call to ask if everything was okay."

"I envy that."

The front door opens, turning us both away from the display on the wall. In comes Luke's mirror image, except he's clean-shaven and he wears his hair longer.

But that smile is similar, and so are the eyes that size me up in no time. "Wow. Do you have a twin sister? If not, let me know when you get tired of this one."

"Kitty, this is my brother, Liam." Luke leans down to hug him before standing back to give me space to shake Liam's hand.

"It's uncanny. And now, I know what you'd look like without a beard." I look from Liam to Luke, eyes narrowed. "I think I like no beard better."

"That's not the only thing you'd like better." Liam winks before continuing into the kitchen, where his mom gives him the same treatment she gave Luke when we arrived.

I turn to Luke with a giggle. "He's a charmer."

"Don't go getting any ideas." But he appears wistful as he looks back toward the articles and pictures on the wall.

In the dining room, I now notice, there's a credenza covered in trophies of all sizes. These are some proud parents.

Mr. Costello joins us, coming up from the basement and looking bewildered. He's a handsome man whose strong bone structure and big, rangy body got passed down to his sons. "I had no idea you all were here. Why doesn't anybody tell me anything?"

"He wears headphones while working in his wood shop," Luke explains. "It drives Mom nuts when he can't hear if she calls him."

Sure enough, I can hear her gentle scolding coming from the kitchen.

I shiver and rub my arms.

Luke notices. "You okay?"

I have to swallow back the lump in my throat. "Missing my parents." So, so much. More than I can say. If I tried to explain I would start crying. And If I stared crying, I might not be able to stop.

He drapes an arm around my shoulders and squeezes in a comforting way. "I'm sorry. Is this too much?"

"No, no." I shake my head hard and force a smile I most definitely don't feel. "No, it's so nice to see. Your family is sweet. And your parents are obviously proud of you."

"Yeah, they're the best." He tucks a thumb under my chin and lifts it. "You're okay? Really?"

"Sure thing." And I am. Sometimes, it hits me when I don't expect it, is all. Sometimes, the pain is as fresh as it ever was, just as fresh as the days and weeks after the accident. Back when I was sure I would never get over it.

And I never did. One doesn't. The pain doesn't go away. A person just learns to live with it.

The banter around the dinner table has me laughing in no time. Mrs. Costello—Marie, she keeps reminding me to call her—made an absolute feast. Two kinds of pasta with meatballs, sausages, spare ribs, and a homemade sauce. It's a good thing there are two fat loaves of bread on the table since the sauce is worthy of sopping up.

"This is extraordinary." I barely have time to say that before going for another bite of meatball, which has to be among the best I've ever tasted. My mom was a good cook, but this is on a whole other level.

"Thank you. I don't get much of an opportunity to cook like this anymore, what with the boys both off on their own and refusing to come home the way they should."

"Mom." Liam rolls his eyes with a laugh. "You wouldn't be happy unless we both moved back in."

"What can I say? I like to be able to keep an eye on my boys." There's a touching amount of fondness in her gaze as she looks at the two of them.

"How's the team looking?" Mr. Costello turns to Luke, eyes twinkling.

"Can we get through one family meal without talking about sports?" Marie gives me an exasperated look.

"As if you're not interested." Liam winks at me. "She's just as big a fan as he is."

"That doesn't mean my entire life has to revolve around it. I see you boys so seldom. When I do, I don't want to talk about the same things we always discuss."

"Our son is on the cusp of moving up in the league." Mr. Costello is clearly proud of his son.

"Aw, thanks, Dad. You know I'm working hard, but it was a team effort. We just won our game at the buzzer."

"That's the way to do it!" his dad cheers.

I look around the table, and Marie is smiling from ear to ear, but I notice Liam is staring down at his plate. I think it must be hard for him not to be able to play. Especially after I saw those pictures and articles. He could've been the hockey star. He's an athlete in his own right, but he might've dreamed of what Luke is so close to achieving.

And that's when I understand it isn't only for himself that Luke works so hard. Not only for his dream. He's also playing for both of them, training for both of them. It's enough to make me want to cry all over again.

"Luke took me skating, and I fell flat on my rear

end after maybe five seconds on the ice," I say to change the subject. "I mean, how is it even possible to stay upright when you're balanced on tiny blades?"

As we all share a laugh at my expense, I catch Luke's appreciative look out of the corner of my eye, and I know it was the right thing to say.

Chapter Seventeen

Why am I a writer? How did I ever get the idea that I should do this for a living. I'm clearly the least talented, most terrible hack who was ever born and this book is shit.

This feeling is nothing new. It just so happens I'm at the same point I always reach in every book—when it seems like the entire thing has been a waste of time and I might as well take up a new career. Happily, it's usually short-lived.

I mean, who would ever want to read this? How can my publisher even consider asking people to pay for this story. It's utter crap.

"Breathe, Kitty." I do that—in through the nose, out through the mouth. Again and again until the idea of burning my laptop and dancing naked around the flaming ashes fades from a very real solution to nothing more than a silly idea I could never get away with. I mean, there's no way I'd ever get my security deposit back, for starters.

Maggie's champing at the bit, too, which isn't helping matters. Nothing like knowing somebody's waiting by their computer for your email to stir the creative juices.

More like, it dries them up completely.

There's a noise at the door. I lift my head from my folded arms and wonder what time it is. It's late afternoon, I see by the clock on my useless laptop. No wonder I'm hungry, though who can eat when it's apparent their life's work was a waste of time and they should be driving for Uber or something like that?

Another noise. Okay, so I didn't imagine it. But what is it? I go to the door and peer out the peep-hole, but I can't see anybody. Though there's still the sound of … is it breathing?

I go down on all fours this time and look under the door. Now, it makes sense. There are four paws out there and one swinging tail, the tip of which I can see moving back and forth.

"Phoebe?" *Is Matt sick again?*

I open the door, ready to greet her, but the sight of a ribbon tied around her neck stops me before I can say a word. Not just a ribbon either. There's also a card tied to it.

"Come on in, girl." After I untie the ribbon, she bounds into the living room and makes herself comfy on the couch. It's been weeks since she's paid a visit, so maybe she was missing me and my apartment.

The card is what I'm more interested in right now. It's blank on the outside, no picture or writing or anything. Inside are three words, scrawled in familiar handwriting: *I'm a dick.*

I have to bite my lip to keep myself from laughing out loud. He's not wrong.

But it isn't an apology either. Telling the truth is telling the truth. That doesn't mean he's sorry for who he is. And that's what I've had the biggest problem with all along.

A dick doesn't stop being a dick just because they know that's who they are. It's not an excuse.

"You're right about that." I stand up, waiting in the doorway for his door to open.

Obviously, he has been watching from the peephole this entire time. Hence my fighting not to laugh.

When the door does open, I'm treated to the sight of a sheepish Matt.

"You like my delivery girl? She gets paid in treats."

"She's worth every single one."

"I am sorry, you know. I really am. What I did was stupid and childish, and I shouldn't have done it." He sticks his hands in his pockets and rocks back and forth on his feet. "I guess I took the protective-neighbor thing a step too far."

"Mmhmm." *What do I say?*

Grandmother is pro-communication, and ordinarily, I'd feel the same way. But this isn't an ordinary situation. No matter how strong I was whenever I imagined this conversation going down—and I imagined it way more times than was probably normal or healthy—when it comes to me looking him straight in the eye and telling it like it is, my tongue forgets how to make words.

"Mmhmm?" His brows lift. "Is that all?"

"It wasn't a protective-neighbor thing, and I think we both know it."

He looks at the floor, telling me I'm right.

"You shouldn't have introduced me to a friend if you didn't like the idea of us actually dating."

"It's not that I don't like the idea of you dating Luke. He's a great guy who's going places. He's exactly the sort of guy you should date. Not some loser or playboy pretender."

I know he's talking about Paxton, who completely rubbed him the wrong way from the beginning. Maybe because Matt had his number from the start. Because he knew about Paxton's past before I did.

"So, what's the problem? You don't like seeing me date anybody, period?"

His head falls back as he groans. "You're not going to make this easy for me, are you?"

"Why should I?"

"Good point." He looks at me again, frowning. "It's been a few weeks, so I guess it's okay to tell you now that, no, I wasn't cool with you dating anybody at all back then."

Back then. I manage to keep a straight face but barely. "Something's changed?"

"Sure. For one thing, I got real with myself. I

didn't think there was any lingering … stuff until you started working again. And dating again."

Stuff, huh? I know what he means even if his way of dancing around things infuriates me.

I'm not making this easy for him, and I can tell he's not thrilled by how quiet I am. What am I supposed to say though? Do I apologize for making him feel icky? For making life hard for him? I have a job to do and a contract, which he so helpfully reminded me of before ever introducing me to his friend.

His hands clench in his pockets. "So, I'm past that now, and I wanted you to know. I'm sorry for making things weird. I don't want things to be weird. Your friendship means a lot."

This I find hard to believe. With a snort, I ask, "Really? Because from where I stand, a lot of our relationship has consisted of you telling me what a dope I am."

"You would see it that way, wouldn't you?"

"You've turned laughing at me into a pastime, Matt."

"I laugh at a lot of people. What I don't do is make a point of hanging around them when I could be doing just about anything else instead. Not that I'm complaining—this isn't a complaint, no matter how much it might sound like one. Besides, friends laugh at each other. They bust balls or make fun or whatever you want to call it. That doesn't mean your friendship doesn't mean something to me.

And when you aren't around, it's obvious how much I like being able to stroll across the hall to ask you a question or see if you want to order lunch."

He has a point there. Life loses some of its color when I don't have anybody to talk to at random times. I know he'll almost always be there during the day. I've come to count on that.

When we aren't speaking, I'm sort of disconnected. Untethered. Back to being alone most of the time, and I don't like it.

"It's nice, having you there," I agree. "I miss what we have when we're fighting."

"So, are we not fighting anymore?"

"I guess we aren't."

Though honestly, there's a part of me that's dying to ask about Ginger. But that would be cruel, and besides, Luke already told me what I needed to know.

I'd like to smack her for hurting him, though I have to wonder if he would ever admit to being hurt. He's a man. In my experience, they don't come right out and admit that sort of thing. They'd rather ... what? Pick up all manner of girls in bars and clubs and bring them home, so they can bang their brains out, I guess?

Is that why he was such a player for so long?

"Not the enthusiasm I was hoping for, but I can't have everything." He looks over my shoulder and shakes his head. "I guess you have a guest. She looks comfortable; I'd hate to move her."

"It's no problem. Besides, I could use the company. I'm tired of talking to myself."

Even though the dog doesn't understand me, speaking out loud to another breathing, living creature sometimes helps. The occasional head tilt I get makes it even better, like she's intrigued by something I've hit on.

I know it's weird, but at times like this, the little things get me through.

"Are you in for the night?" I venture. "Wanna order dinner?"

The momentary crinkling of his forehead tells me I'm about to be turned down. My heart sinks before he even opens his mouth. "Uh, no, sorry. I have plans tonight."

Be his friend. Be his friend, damn it. "Oh? A date?" I wiggle my eyebrows up and down to show I'm perfectly, absolutely, a hundred percent fine with him dating somebody. Because I am. I totally am.

This is me being fine with it.

"Yeah, sort of. Nothing serious. We met a few weeks ago—"

Our eyes meet. *Oh, jeez, why am I constantly tested in this way?*

"A few weeks ago? Like, when you went out with Luke that night?"

"Actually, yes. We've, uh, gone to her place since then. I didn't think you'd want to hear …"

I sincerely wish I could control my penchant for blushing. Like if a magical fairy came down from the heavens right this very minute, I wouldn't even ask for a decent ending for my book, which is saying something since I'm at my wits' end with it and I could use all the help I can get.

No. I'd much rather be able to control my blushing. Especially right now, in this situation.

"That's nice of you. I mean, I didn't hear anything that night, but if you think it's a problem, I appreciate you being considerate."

His gaze flicks over me.

Am I believable? Is he going to call me out? Oh, please, please, don't let him pursue this. I don't feel like talking about how I made no effort whatsoever to be quiet that night.

Meanwhile, my cheeks are hotter than ever. *If I heard her, he must've heard me. Is he going to be cool for once? Is he going to act like he didn't hear? Or will he hint—or much worse—flat-out tell me he knows what I sound like when I orgasm?*

Maybe it was easier when we weren't speaking to each other.

"I'm glad we didn't disturb you then." He has a gleam in his eye, and I know he's trying not to make fun of me. "So, you wouldn't mind if we came back here then? We wouldn't disturb you when you're working?"

"Please. I would welcome the disruption right now. I'm stuck, big time."

"Oh, really? You're at that part now?"

He really does know me well.

"Maybe you should put your work aside for a while and get out. Get some air. It's a beautiful day."

"Maybe," I say with a shrug. I'm really not sure what I want to do right now between Luke, Matt, and my book. I decide to change the subject. "Hey, they're playing a game tomorrow night. Wanna come? I could use some insight into game strategy."

That was a mistake. I can tell when his forehead crinkles again. "Um, I can't make any promises. I might have another date."

"Of course. Have fun."

"Oh, I intend to." He grins and whistles for Phoebe to follow him as he opens the door.

I wish I could smile.

I wish there weren't this sense of something unspoken hanging between us, an invisible elephant in the hall. We can walk past it, slide around it, but it's there. Still waiting to be acknowledged.

Chapter Eighteen

THE ENERGY IS different this evening. I can feel it as soon as I walk through the doors and find a seat with the other girls, down by the Plexiglass.

I know why it's different too. Luke said his coach told the representatives that some of the players looked like they were ready to move up in the league, and they want to perform at their best.

"This could be the night," Darcy reminds me as I sit next to her.

"I know. It's amazing I got any sleep last night."

Granted, there were a few reasons why I tossed and turned. Luke and his future were definitely part of it.

So was my complete ineptitude as a writer. Yes, I have writer's block on where to go, on how to make things better. And wondering if I should come up with a new career.

And then there was that tiny fact that there was a girl next door with Matt! I stared at the ceiling for half the night. At least, that's how it feels right now, dragging my feet in spite of the excitement over the game.

"I think this is it for Luke and Mark. I really do." Darcy's practically hugging herself; she's so excited.

"Let's hope." My fingers are crossed.

It's obvious from the second the puck hits the ice that the players know what's at stake here. Immediately, bodies crash into bodies, sticks clashing. I wince when Luke takes a check from the other team's center that sends him reeling back.

"Holy cow," I mutter. My heart's in my throat. This is going to be a tough game.

And it is. It's violent, it's hard, and the other team might even be playing dirty. I can't count the number of times Darcy and the other girls scream at the referees for doing nothing about the repeated checks going on.

"What, are they blind?" she shrieks, throwing her hands into the air.

I'm right there with her. It's like there was an agreement before the start of the game to look the other way.

It's taking a toll on the team, obviously. They're playing tough but with the same sort of desperation I saw when they fell behind during the first game I came to. They're making mistakes—even I can see that, and I've only just learned the game in the last few weeks. Missing passes and making errors.

And they're getting more aggressive with each minute. At least the refs aren't calling them on it and ignoring the other team. It's like they might as well not be out there.

Luke is managing to keep his cool. He isn't letting himself get pulled into a fight like he did before. Instead, he's all over the ice, trying to pick up the slack. By the end of the first period, the game is tied at one apiece.

"I have a bad feeling about this game."

Nobody hears me murmuring, which is probably for the best. I don't want anybody to think I'm a spoilsport. But fists are bound to start flying soon, and it's not going to be pretty.

The second period isn't much easier to watch than the first. The players are starting to get tired from all the aggressive, high-speed playing. I'd bet their frustration with the refs isn't helping matters. It's hard to do something right, to play by the rules, when the other team is doing whatever they want.

The score is stuck at one goal each in the last few minutes of the second period. The goalies are working their butts off out there. My heart's racing when a bunch of players pile up at our goal with the other team trying desperately to put the puck in the net.

It's such a relief when somebody knocks the puck away, bringing it around behind the net and waiting for another player to open up and take it farther down the ice.

Mark's about ready to take it.

Only one of the other team's players has other ideas.

Except something goes very wrong. There is still

a tangle of players and sticks near the net.

The result is an absolute nightmare. The other player knocks Mark down, and then he lands straight on his leg moments later.

I swear, I hear a snap.

"Oh my God!" I cover my mouth with my hands, jumping to my feet in horror.

Everybody around me does the same thing. There are more than a few cries of dismay and shock from around the arena.

That's not what brings tears to my eyes though.

It's the sound of Mark groaning and grunting and almost screaming in agony out on the ice. He's reaching for his leg, his face beet red, teeth bared.

The coach bolts onto the ice along with the referees. Both teams mill around, watching, some of them turning away when they see the mangled mess that is Mark's leg. The player who landed on him is nearby, and one glance tells me how horrified he is by what happened. He probably feels terrible about it. I know I would.

Ginger's in hysterics. The girls near her try to keep her calm, hugging her and stroking her hair, but there's no easing her right now. I can't blame her.

Luke's out there, lingering near Mark, giving the team doctors space, but watching just the same. He looks worried, putting it mildly. Even sick.

He looks up into the stands, searching. He finds me. The slight shake of his head speaks volumes.

Not that I necessarily needed that confirmation of things being very, very bad.

I'm no doctor, but legs aren't supposed to twist like Mark's did. I can't even look for too long, or I feel all dizzy and faint, and I don't consider myself to have a weak stomach.

There's an announcement over the system, but I can hardly hear it. Not because of the noise from the other fans—in fact, the place has gone painfully silent. Who can cheer and have a conversation and be obnoxious when someone is in agony?

Ginger works her way down the row, followed by a couple of her close friends.

"Where do you think she's going?" I ask nobody in particular.

"Probably to the locker room—or straight to the hospital. I mean, what can they do for him in the locker room? He'll need an X-ray at the very least." Darcy's right. An X-ray is the very least of what he needs right now.

And it's not just his leg I'm thinking about. If he wants to move up as much as Luke does, this will kill him. Even if he heals up completely and quickly, he'll probably have to wait until next season.

"They can't possibly play the rest of the game," I whisper, looking back down to the ice.

The teams have retreated to their benches to regroup.

We're sitting close to our team's bench, and I

can hear what's going on down there. It's not the coach talking to the players.

It's Luke. He's stepping up, rallying them. "He'd want you all to keep playing as hard and as focused as you can. If he finds out we ended up losing this game after he played his guts out, he'll never forgive us."

He points a finger at each of them. "And don't think I won't name names because I will. Even if his knee is completely fucked, you know he'll kick the shit out of every one of you with his good leg the second he's out of the hospital. So, get out there and play your best. Watch each other's backs and remember all the time we've put in together."

It's rousing. It's inspiring. I would throw myself at him right here and now if we weren't separated by rows of seats and, you know, in public and whatnot. Otherwise, he wouldn't be able to get away from me.

He scores within thirty seconds of the period starting. Then, Greg scores and then Mike. By the time it's all over, the score is four to one, and the girls around me are weeping since this was all done for Mark. They managed to rally in spite of exhaustion and frustration and concern for their friend.

I get why people are so passionate about sports. Why they treat it like it's such a big deal, why they idolize the players. I don't think I've ever seen a team so downtrodden, so near the point of snapping, come back to win in such definitive fashion.

And I'm crying, too, since Luke managed to pull everybody together.

But poor Mark.

Luke doesn't take long to come out of the locker room. His hair is wet, his clothes damp, like he put them straight on when he got out of the shower. "I've gotta get to the hospital."

"I know. I'll come with you, if you want."

"No, no. It's okay. We had those plans with Hayley and her boyfriend, remember?"

Right. I completely forgot we were supposed to get together for dinner tonight. "I can come with you for a while. I don't want you to have to go through this alone."

"I won't be alone. I'll have the rest of the team with me. It'll probably be better for you girls to stay behind anyway. There's gonna be a lot of us there." He stops at the front door and kisses me, but he's distracted. Distant.

"Let me know how things go, please. I'll be waiting by the phone." Before putting him in a cab, I add, "And tell Ginger I said I hope things go okay."

He nods, giving me a meaningful look. "Yeah, we'll see how long she sticks around after this."

Ouch. I didn't even think about that. I'd defend her, but he knows her better than I do. Besides, he's in a huge hurry.

It's not until he's halfway down the block that I realize I forgot to congratulate him on the win.

Chapter Nineteen

"God, that sounds terrible." Hayley's looking pale by the time I finish describing what happened at the game. I can relate since even thinking about it turns my stomach.

"I'm sure Luke wanted to meet you tonight. He couldn't bring himself to leave the hospital. Everybody's waiting there to hear how the surgery went."

She nods her head. "Of course. I'm sure he would've been there mentally even if he had come to dinner. Are you sure you don't want to be there with him though?"

"He insisted. Besides, there are just so many of them already—the team, I mean. I think most of the girls went home."

"Except Ginger."

"I guess." All I can do is think about what Luke said. She wants to be married to a big leaguer, and Mark was on his way up. But what if he never plays again? What does that mean? "Anyway, he texted before I left home to say the surgery was going okay, according to updates through some app they use at the hospital now. But it won't be over for another hour or two."

"Damn. That doesn't sound like something a person can easily bounce back from."

"No, it doesn't."

And she didn't see it. I can't bring myself to think about it anymore. I don't want Hayley's boyfriend to have a bad impression of the girl who puked in the middle of dinner because she couldn't stop thinking about a guy's leg turned the wrong way.

Hayley's facing the restaurant's front door. When her face lights up, I know a certain special someone has arrived. She waves him over, and I swear, I've never seen her like this. Her eyes are so bright, her smile just a quarter inch away from being downright goofy. If that.

She's in love. Really and truly.

"Hey you," she greets a tall blond man who could easily be on the cover of a magazine.

He's basically her male equivalent, meaning I don't know whether to salivate or fall at his feet or what. His tan is deeply impressive. He has the body of somebody who plays sports—at least for fun. Is it wrong that I want to ask if he surfs out in California? Surely, not everybody surfs out there.

His blue eyes sparkle when he looks down at her, his hands cupping her shoulders. The way he smiles at her! It's like she's the only person in the world.

All of a sudden, I feel sort of bad for being here.

"Hey you," he whispers before kissing her forehead.

A forehead kiss. Oh my God. That's the swoon-worthiest of all kisses. Does he know what he's doing to my romantic heart?

Finally, he notices me. Not that I'm about to complain. "Sorry! She tends to take up all the space in my brain whenever I see her. Nicholas Donnelly." He extends a hand to shake, his smile warm and charming.

"Kitty Valentine."

"Hayley has told me a lot about you." He glances at her and then at me again.

"I promise, none of it is true."

Hayley snorts. "What if I told him you're the best writer in the world?"

"The world? What about the entire galaxy?"

Nicholas laughs. "She said you were modest too. About as modest as she is, if I remember correctly." His mouth screws up in a knowing smirk when he turns to her.

"I didn't say any such thing!" She swats him with her napkin, giggling helplessly. "You've been here ten seconds, and you're stirring up trouble already."

He grins my way from across the table. "Can I tell you a secret?"

Can he tell me a secret? We've known each other less than half a minute, and I didn't know his last name until just now. The playfulness in his smile, in his voice, makes me want to play along though. That, and knowing how much Hayley cares about him.

"Of course. I love secrets."

"I've read all of your books over the last several weeks."

My jaw makes a clunking sound when it hits the table. Or is that in my head?

Even Hayley looks surprised. "You have? When have you had time for that?"

"I made the time." He looks pained though when he turns back to me. "Is that okay? Do you mind? It's just that Hayley told me so much about you and talks about you all the time, so I figured I should get an idea for myself of what you write."

"Wow. I bet you thought it was juvenile compared to the work you do every day."

"Juvenile? Hell no!" He stares at me like he doesn't quite believe it. "No, that was the last word on my mind. You rekindled my love of reading. I was always a bookworm when I was a kid, but I haven't had a lot of time for pleasure reading over the last ... ten years or so." He and Hayley share a knowing laugh.

"So, you enjoyed yourself?" This is so awkward. So painfully awkward. Not because he was kind enough to read my work, but because we're sitting here and talking about it. I have to fight the impulse to cringe.

"I'll be honest." He folds his hands on the table, meeting me head-on with a blank expression but it doesn't last long. He winks, followed by a slow smile. "I wouldn't have brought it up if I didn't like your books. I wouldn't have kept buying them either."

That's a relief, but I'm still in shock. "You didn't buy them all, did you? No way."

"Yes way." He reaches into his pocket and pulls out his phone. "Check it out."

Sure enough, there's a photo of a stack of books on what's obviously a hotel room nightstand. Nobody would decorate their actual bedroom like that.

"Wow. You are dedicated." I'm at a loss for words after that, so I decide on, "Thank you."

"Thank you. Like I said, I feel like reading again just because I like it. Not because I have to."

Hayley shrugs, leaning against him. He drapes an arm around her shoulders. "What can I say? The man goes above and beyond."

"It means a lot to me to get to know somebody who's so important to Hayley." He says it like it's the simplest, most commonsense thing in the world. He did it because he knew it would matter to her.

Dang it. I'm not going to lie. If I hadn't liked him coming out of this dinner, it might've made things easier for me. Sure, I want Hayley to be happy. I want her to have everything she wants.

But I want the man she chooses to be right for

her. To be a good, stand-up sort of guy. She needs that, and she deserves it.

If he rubbed me the wrong way, if he seemed too smug or a little dismissive, or if he didn't smile graciously at the server when he ordered a bottle of wine, I could've hoped she would see the truth about him being wrong and rested easy, knowing she wasn't moving to California anytime soon.

That's just not the case. She isn't only enamored with him—that much is clear as dinner goes on and they practically finish each other's thoughts. They already have that special rhythm, like they've rehearsed our conversation in advance and they can prompt each other to keep things flowing. It's adorable.

And sad. It's sad for me; I can't help it. I'm only human. I would never try to hold her back, especially now that I see how happy she is, how completely natural they seem together. When I can literally spot the goose bumps that pop up on her arm when he brushes the back of her hand with his fingers.

But I'm sad for myself. We've been a physical part of each other's lives since college. She's my other half. FaceTime is great and everything, and naturally, we could visit, but it'd never be the same.

Nothing would be the same.

I wish Matt were here. He would understand. He might even nudge me under the table or pat my leg to show me he knew what I was going through. Because he would. He always does. I try to push

Matt back out of my head and continue the lively conversation with Hayley and Nicholas.

After dinner and a long kiss good-bye with Hayley, Nicholas heads off to meet a college friend, who's getting married, for drinks. Hayley said she'd catch up with him in a bit. I know she's dying to hear my first impression of him.

"So? What do you think?"

I purse my lips, eyes narrowed. "He's nice."

"Just nice?" Her voice is flat. Flat like the palm of her hand, which I just know she's dying to sweep across my cheek. Like I need sense slapped into me.

"Yeah, he's nice." I polish off my drink and manage to swallow without choking on my laughter.

"You're so mean!" She just about pushes me off my barstool. Once we were finished eating, we decided to move over to the bar to have one more drink before she heads out with Nicholas.

"Okay, fine. He's outstanding. He's gorgeous, funny, smart. Sweet," I add when I remember how he read my books.

"He's the best. I knew you would see that when you met him." My best friend chews her lip, still worried. "You're not just saying that, are you? Because you know it'll make me happy?"

"Look me in the eyes and tell me you think I would lie about liking somebody if I honestly didn't for some reason. Like if my gut told me there was something off. I care too much about you to hold back. You know that."

"You wouldn't just say that to spare my feelings?"

I shoot her a look. "Babe, I can see how this is going to go. This is a real-deal sort of relationship." I reach out to take her face in my hands. "I am very, very happy for you. I want this for you."

"Even if it means me leaving?"

This isn't so easy. I have to fight hard against the pressure in my chest, behind my eyes. "Yes. Even if it means you leaving."

Her eyes get watery. I can feel the same thing happening to me. "But I don't want to leave you. And I couldn't ask you to come."

"I can visit all the time. You know I can work from anywhere in the whole world, right? You'll get sick of me after a while, when you're busy trying to set up a life with Nicholas."

"I could never get sick of you." Tears spill onto her cheeks. "I love you too much."

"I love you too."

And we're hugging, and we're crying, and we're in the middle of a restaurant bar with people all around us, probably wondering who broke up with who and whether we could both use another drink to soothe our pain.

No amount of drinking will soothe my pain; I know that much. I've tried it in the past, and it just hasn't worked out so well.

That doesn't mean I can't try again.

Only when I get home, I find I don't have much alcohol to choose from.

And when I go across the hall, barefoot and in sweats, to ask whether Matt has some wine, there's no answer when I knock. He's out with his girl, whoever she is.

Looks like I'm alone for real.

Chapter Twenty

I WALK INTO Luke's Saturday morning practice for a chance to see him and sit down next to Darcy.

"It'll take tons of rehab before he's able to get back on the ice." Darcy's hands shake as she brushes tears away. "He was so close to having everything he wanted. He worked so hard."

"I'm crushed for him. To think, everything changed like that." I snap my fingers with a sigh. "I guess that's true for all of us. Everything can change in no time, over the stupidest reasons."

Like my parents. They've been on my heart ever since I had dinner with Luke's family a couple of weeks ago. Not that they're ever very far away from my thoughts, but they've been closer to the forefront lately.

If they hadn't been out walking at that exact time.

If they had taken just another fifteen seconds before leaving the apartment.

If they had decided to stay home instead.

And let's not even get started on the drunk driver and the decisions he could've made that would've spared lives that night. If he hadn't blown through that intersection and run my parents down.

I went from being a normal teenager with two parents, who were kind of strict about grades and curfew, to an orphan in no time.

She musters a smile. "At least they won. And Luke looked great out there. He saved the day."

"I wanted to congratulate him for that, but he's been sort of MIA since the game. He did let me know when Mark's surgery was finished, but he went home after that. I haven't spoken to him much today."

He's out on the ice right now, practicing, in his own world, away from the rest of the team.

I wonder what he's thinking about. I wish he would tell me.

"I'm sure it shook him up. I know the whole team's feeling it. I mean, that could've been them. Any of them."

"That's true. I imagine they must have a lot of mixed emotions getting back on the ice."

"Part of being one of us girls is knowing how to manage situations like this—I don't know if you wanna put it in your book or what, but it's something to keep in mind if you're in this for the long haul."

Oof. That hits me in a funny sort of way. I don't know how to feel about the thought of being in this for the long haul. I certainly didn't go into this with the idea of extending it any further than a few weeks of dating.

Shoot. Would it make me look like a horrible person if I walked away? Like, *Hey, thanks for the good times. I have everything I need?*

I have to pull myself out of my questions and turn my attention back to Darcy. "What do you mean?"

She shrugs, looking out to where the guys are running drills. "Giving them the space they need to process things while being there if they need help. Walking that fine line between support and smothering."

"Gotcha. How do you manage it?"

"I say, *I'm here for you if you need to talk about it.* Sometimes, we end up talking. Sometimes, not. But once I put it out there, I don't push. It only annoys him if I push too hard."

"It sounds like you have a solid plan in place."

Her lips twitch. "Yeah, well, trial and error."

I want to ask if she'd be willing to share more, but the thought of being called a user—or worse—holds me back. I decide to turn my focus back on the practice. The assistant coach has them running drills now, and I keep my eyes on Luke, who has no trouble keeping up.

Out of the corner of my eye, I see the head coach jogging down the stairs from his office. When he joins the team on the ice, he gets everyone's attention, even the few of us in the stands. We all quiet down, but we can't hear what he's saying.

When a cheer rings out and everybody starts playfully shoving and clapping Luke on the back, I know.

"He got the call! He got the call!" Darcy throws her arms around me and screams in my ear until it rings, but that's okay. I'm screaming, too, along with everybody else in the stands.

Is it true?

Luke finds me and skates over at top speed. He's beaming, overjoyed, and now, I'm sure.

"COME ON. ANOTHER round!" One of the other guys from the team—is it Donny or Joey—throws his arms into the air, and everybody cheers.

For once, Luke is letting himself go. He's not so disciplined when he receives the happiest news of his life, I guess, and who could tell him to behave otherwise?

I couldn't be happier for him.

What gives me pause though and keeps me from joining in the festivities is the way everybody's roping me into this. Congratulating me like I had anything to do with the good news. I've known the man, what, a few weeks, and they're practically throwing me a party?

I don't deserve that. Even if I'd known him my entire life, I wouldn't deserve it.

They don't seem to agree.

"Come on! Another drink!" Darcy presses a glass into my hand. She's tipsy, maybe even slightly beyond, and it's barely noon.

"No, thanks. One of us should stay clearheaded." When she pouts, I have no choice but to give in. "Fine. I'll nurse it."

"That's more like it." She finishes her beer before picking up another from the bar. "You know, I envy you. I already did, but now, I do even more."

"Hey now. Why would you envy me? I'm just a normal person. You should know that by now."

"Yeah, but look what you have. You've got a man who's about to move up in the league. Do you know what I'd do if Bobby got a new contract?" She holds up her left hand and points to the ring finger. "I'd lock him down. Then, I'd quit my job. Don't get me wrong!" I'm laughing, but she shakes me to pull my attention back to her. "I love teaching. I love the kids. But if I could, if Bobby made enough money, I'd be out of there so quick."

"I know it must be a stressful job, being a teacher."

"It's stressful, being a hockey wife too."

Wow, she's making a pretty big jump here, taking me from a casual fling to a hockey wife, but I decide to play along. I want to hear what she has to say. "How's it stressful?"

"He'll always be on the road, for one thing. So, unless you're really secure with him and have faith in him, that could lead to trouble. Not that I think he would ever cheat!" She grabs my arm, glaring at me in what I know she thinks is a reassuring manner but is most definitely not. It's almost creepy actually.

"I'm sure he wouldn't."

"Then, there's the social commitments the hockey wives and girlfriends have. There's all kinds of charity events. They're really active in the community."

"That's nice. I'm glad they do that."

"But it takes up a lot of time, I heard, and you're already such a busy person." Her eyes widen. "Unless you stop writing! You'd be able to afford to do that by then." She says this with all the wonder of a kid discovering presents on Christmas morning.

"Okay, okay, I think we're getting ahead of ourselves. He doesn't even have a contract yet." Not that I'm trying to rain on everybody's parade, but I'm surprised Darcy isn't wondering what our children will think of Daddy being on the road all the time.

"Hey, it's okay if you're not sure you can handle it. There's so much to consider."

I can tell she's trying to keep my face in focus, but she's having a hard time with it.

I have to excuse myself. Anything to get away from these expectations. Everybody assumes I'm in it for the long haul, especially now that things are looking better than ever for Luke.

Now, that would make me a user. It would make me a terrible person if I latched on to him now when I had no intention of doing so. I like him a lot, of course, but there's nothing about us that gives me long-term vibes.

Especially now that I've seen Hayley and Nicholas together. Sure, they're still in that relationship bubble, where everything's wonderful and nothing in the world matters more than the two of them. But they have a spark. They have that connection. They're completely fascinated with each other, and they have a ton of common ground to pull from.

They're willing to sacrifice for each other. Nicholas hinted last night that he likes New York. A lot. Enough to consider moving here. And I know she's already considering moving for his sake.

Would I do that for Luke? Honestly?

The thought hasn't crossed my mind.

No, I wouldn't want to move someplace else for him. I can't imagine it. We just aren't … there. And we never will be.

Here I am, as usual, about to do the opposite of what any sane person in my situation would do. Most girls would hook their man right here and now. He has nothing but good things ahead of him, right?

Instead, I'm going to break it off with him.

He's in the center of a huge group of people, some of who I've never seen before. They aren't even part of the team. Maybe they're his outside friends, or maybe they're complete strangers—I have no idea. All I know is, Luke is the star. And he deserves to be.

But no, there's no place for me at his side. I don't belong in this world. I could never make hockey or any single sport my life.

It'll be better to end things soon.

I only hope he doesn't resent me too much for it.

When he catches my eye and waves me over, I join him. But it's with a heavy heart.

Chapter Twenty-One

"I CAN'T WAIT to get you upstairs and tear your clothes off." Luke's hand is on my butt as we climb the stairs.

Oh boy. He's feeling on top of the world. As he should.

But this isn't going to end well.

"I think it would be better if you rested and drank a lot of water. Like, a gallon at least." I have to keep things light while holding myself at arm's length. Because it would be wrong to have one last go-round when I know I'm going to break up with him.

Right? It would totally be wrong to indulge myself in him just one … last … time …

Down, girl. Stay focused.

Besides, the man is in no condition. He's stumbling up the stairs, drunk as a skunk. While Luke is in peak physical condition, I'm not sure he could perform to the best of his abilities in this situation.

He flops down on the sofa once we're in the apartment and kicks off his shoes. "I can't believe it. I mean, you work your whole life for something, and then *bam*, it's right there in front of you." He holds out a hand, palm up, like he's balancing his hockey career there.

"I suppose it's a bit overwhelming." I place a bottle of water in his hand. "Here. Do yourself a favor."

But he's too busy marveling over his good fortune to care about how rotten he'll feel later. "All this time. All this time! And finally, it's gonna happen. I mean, it has to happen. I'm so close."

"You just got called up. It's happening. You deserve this." I take a seat at the other end of the sofa and pull my legs up under me. "Have you called your parents?"

"Of course. Mom wants to throw a big party. Dad has probably already told the whole neighborhood."

"I'm sure everybody is proud of you. The whole team will come for the party, and they'll carry you on their shoulders down the street and everything."

I expect him to grin over this, maybe elaborate on the idea. Instead, he frowns. "That isn't funny."

"I wasn't trying to be. I mean, I was only kidding around."

The frown deepens into a scowl. "It sounded like you were making fun of me."

"That's the last thing I wanted to do. I didn't mean it to come out that way."

Boy, he can turn on a dime—and not only on the ice. It's a good thing he doesn't do much drinking if this is how he acts when he's drunk.

"There's nothing wrong with my neighborhood being proud."

"Luke, I didn't say there was. What's the matter? You went from being so happy to sounding angry."

He looks away, toward the window. His jaw twitches. "I don't know. Sorry. I'm mixed up. It wasn't until you said that … I mean, what about …"

I wait, expecting him to continue. When he doesn't, I clear my throat. "What about what? Why are you upset?"

More jaw twitching. His nostrils flare. His brows draw together over that twice-broken nose of his. "I was thinking about Mark. You said the whole team, and his face popped up in my head."

Oh. I sigh, reaching for his hand. "What happened to him … you couldn't have helped him. You couldn't have stopped it. I don't know why these things happen, but they do. You can't hold yourself responsible, and you can't let this overshadow your happiness."

"Would you be able to be happy and excited when your friend was in the hospital? It's clear he's never gonna play like he used to."

"I am so sorry to hear that. I know how much he wanted this too."

"What if it had been me?" His eyes meet mine, and the worry in them touches me deeply. He's like a child in a man's body. So scared, so guilty. So aware of how close he came to having his dreams wiped away.

"It wasn't you though. It wasn't meant to be that way."

He scoffs, "Just like it wasn't me that night. When Liam … wanted to get home early after practice to watch a game on TV. I wanted to stick around for a while. He got a ride home with another kid whose brother was picking him up. They ended up injured but not badly. And Liam's never walked again."

"Luke, it wasn't your fault."

"I could've convinced him to stay with me. And Mark. I knew he was playing too hard on Saturday. Trying to be a hero, wanting to impress the reps. He wasn't paying attention. I should've warned him to pay better attention."

"You didn't have the chance to do it. Would he have even listened? He was desperate to get noticed."

"Yeah, and look where it left him." He scrubs his hands through his hair, grunting. "Why am I the one? Why do I get to keep playing hockey? Why am I not the one who got hurt? Why is this happening to me?"

Whew, boy. He gets deep when he's drunk. To think, I imagined our big conversation revolving around me ending things, which was what I had planned to eventually do after explaining that I never intended to get sucked into his world.

"Can I offer a gentle suggestion? And I'm begging you, please don't take this the wrong way." Maybe that's too much to ask when he's drunk, but I have to try. "You might want to consider talking to somebody. A therapist. They can help you work these things out."

His face hardens. "A therapist?"

"Yeah. You're carrying a heavy burden right now, and you don't deserve it. They could help you work out your feelings, so you wouldn't feel guilty. Like I said, it's only a suggestion."

He sits up straighter, snorting. "Yeah, right. I'll go into therapy."

There was a fifty-fifty shot that he'd take it the wrong way, so I'm not entirely surprised by his reaction. "I'm sorry if that upset you. I only care about you being able to enjoy all the good things in your life without feeling bad about them."

"Sorry. I can't see myself doing that."

"It's completely up to you."

He heaves a sigh, shoulders sagging. He's looking pathetic and guilt is written all over his face. I feel sorry for him. Something tells me that even if he does end up with a contract—and he should; honestly, he's an incredible athlete and dedicated to his sport—he won't be truly, deep-down happy. He'll always carry this with him. He'll always wonder why he gets to be the one all these good things happen to.

"I think we should call it quits."

Whoa. Wait up.

"Huh?"

"Don't take it the wrong way." He glances at me from the corner of his eye. "I don't want you to think I'm dropping you right after I got good news."

"No, I don't think that."

"It's just …" He sighs again. "It's just that I don't expect you to ever be one of those girls. The ones who make hockey their life. Or football or baseball or whatever. You have your own life and your career, and that's great. I wouldn't want you to take time away from that."

He has an interesting way of twisting things around; I'll give him that.

He's the generous guy, isn't he? Wouldn't want me to take time away from my life. What he's actually saying is he wants a girl who's going to give him everything. All of her time, her attention, her devotion. Somebody who'll make his life her life. His dreams, her dreams.

And he's right. I'm not that person. I'd rather walk side by side with a man, both of us having dreams and goals of our own, which we help each other with, than maintain a one-sided relationship, where all of my energy is poured into somebody else.

No, thank you.

"I understand. Thanks for being honest."

He waits. I get the feeling he's expecting more.

"Thank you for letting me into your world," I venture. Is that enough?

"It's been great. And I hope you got everything you needed for your book."

"Oh, for sure. I'm about to wrap it up actually. I'll send it over to my editor sometime this week."

"I'll look for it when it comes out." He stands and then wobbles. "Shit. I had too much to drink."

"Why don't you chill for a while? No hard feelings or anything."

"Thank you," he says.

I leave the sofa to him and sit down at my desk. He stretches out, and within minutes, the sound of his soft snoring fills the air.

He's a nice guy. But he's a lot to deal with too. I'm glad I didn't have to be the one to break things off. Here I was, worried he would call me all sorts of names, the way the hero in my book did to my heroine when she got scared and tried to back off, tried to cool things down between them.

Really, she was only doing it for his sake, but he didn't see it that way. Rather than accept the fact that she wanted to protect his career and his image, he took it as evidence that she'd used his name to boost her popularity as a journalist. Once she'd earned some respect from her colleagues, he thought, she'd decided it was time to dump him and move on to somebody with an even more talent.

Now, I'm at the end. Where they'll have their

big moment. Where he'll read the article she wrote, explaining to her readers how much he means to her. How none of her success matters without him.

Yes, I know that would never happen in real life. There are a hundred reasons why such a gesture wouldn't fly. But I write fiction, so I'm allowed to create situations that wouldn't exactly take place in real life. I mean, is happily ever after guaranteed in real life?

No, but it is in romance. Which is why her editor lets her get away with publishing such a piece and why the love of her life reads it and understands she was never using him. It's what reminds him of what he loves best about her. Her bravery, her willingness to put it all on the line, no matter how foolish she might look.

Is there a tear in my eye as I work? Maybe. Maybe more than a single tear.

A text from Matt pulls me out of the world of my book. *Just got a call from one of the guys on the team. Is it true? Did Luke get called up?*

Word travels fast.

He did. He's currently passed out on my couch since he broke up with me and tried to leave and I told him to chill out. I'd lost track of how many beers they'd bought him today.

He sends a handful of I'm thinking emojis with the finger and the thumb against the chin. *Is he really out cold?*

I look over at Luke. His mouth is slightly open, and drool is starting to leak from the corner.

Um, yeah. He's dead to the world.

Can I come over and mess with him? I promise it won't be anything bad. He did it to me once.

What is it with guys wanting to mess with each other when they're passed out?

Okay, I text back, biting my lip to keep from giggling too loudly. *But be quiet. And don't ruin my furniture.*

Chapter Twenty-Two

I've never seen anyone calmer and in complete control as my grandmother is on her wedding day.

I mean, I'm not even the one about to get hitched, and I'm about ready to ask if she has any sedatives around. "Did the caterer find everything in the kitchen?" I ask her current butler, Frank, in passing. He's younger than Peter by a great many years, and honestly, he's much better suited to the position.

Not that Peter can't handle things, but she keeps her staff on their toes. I suspect the only reason Peter stayed in that position so long was the feelings that had already developed between them.

"Yes, everything's proceeding according to plan. The guests have started to arrive."

"Already?" A glance at the nearest clock tells me they're right on time since we're about thirty minutes away from the start of the ceremony. This day has absolutely blown by. That's always how it goes when there are major, important things happening.

If I were just lying around the apartment—or

worse, struggling through a difficult scene? Time would crawl on its belly. Meanwhile, when there's a deadline looming, the whole day can pass in the blink of an eye.

Why am I so nervous? It's a good kind of nervousness at least. There isn't any dread in it. I know my grandmother would never do anything she wasn't fully, completely ready to do.

"Kathryn, for heaven's sake, would you settle down? Everything is going perfectly well." She sits in front of her vanity table, adding the final touch with a string of pearls at her throat.

"I feel it's my duty as your maid of honor to double-check. It's not like you'd let me perform any of the normal duties."

Her eyes meet mine in the mirror. "Forgive me if the notion of visiting a strip club is a bit beyond me."

"God forbid I make a joke. Like I would ever in a million years visit a place like that … with you," I add.

She snickers. "Now, I wish I had taken you up on it. You know how I enjoy watching you cringe."

"I knew it! I knew you did things on purpose to make my skin crawl."

She laughs softly before touching up her lipstick. "It's a grandmother's privilege to embarrass her granddaughter at every given opportunity. You blush so easily."

"Thanks. I know that." And right on cue, there's

warmth in my cheeks. "Any other pearls of wisdom you want to pass down on this special day?"

She turns on her dressing stool and looks me up and down. "Well, now that your dress and hair fit you well, I see you've learned those two pearls," she says with a wink.

"That's it? Make sure my dresses fit and my hairstyle shows off my shoulders? Those are the keys to life?"

"There are other keys, but those are two of them. Know what fits you best, know what suits you best. Don't be afraid to stick to what you know works, trends be damned. Look at me. I've found what I like and made it work for me all these years."

"Including your soon-to-be husband."

"Hush." She clicks her tongue, standing. "You are too much, and I don't know why I bother."

I can hear voices coming from downstairs. "It's filling up down there. Are you nervous?"

"No, and stop trying to make it otherwise." She holds a corsage of pale pink and cream roses against her chest. "What do you think?"

"That looks nice." I help her pin it on and breathe in the scent of her perfume. That's another thing that's never changed. I can't smell Chanel No. 5 without thinking about her.

"Would you like to know why I'm not nervous?"

I nod, looking up from her flowers.

"Because I know exactly what and who I want.

I've removed everyone from my life who doesn't line up with who I am. I owe them nothing. I owe much more to myself."

"That's so easy to say. Not so easy to practice."

"I've had fifty extra years to practice." She pats my hand. "Your time will come."

I have to wonder.

"Trust me, I know what I'm doing. And the people I've invited to watch me exchange vows with the man I love support our union. They're true friends who want nothing more than for us to declare our commitment and rejoice in it." Her happy sigh is what comes close to squeezing tears from my eyes.

But dang it, I worked like hell on my makeup, and I won't ruin it. Though waterproof mascara might've been a good investment for today. I was too busy worrying whether we'd ordered enough sausage puffs from the caterer for the reception.

Before we head downstairs, I have to get something off my chest. "Listen," I whisper, taking her hands before picking up my bouquet, "I want to tell you how happy I am for you. Not just today, but always. You two deserve this love, and I hope you have so many more years of it."

"Thank you, my sweet Kathryn." She presses her cheek to mine rather than kissing so she doesn't smear her lipstick. "You've given me so much, simply by being my granddaughter. Someone to be proud of. Someone to look forward to seeing every week. And I look forward to watching you find this for yourself. The comfort of a real, true love. Because that's what love is between two people who've decided to devote their lives to their union. Not to each other, mind you—that's a misconception. My life is not devoted to Peter. It's devoted to us, together, our life. Which means, I must take care of myself as well to make certain I'm the best I can be for us. In return, I have the comfort of knowing I don't have to go through life alone. No matter what happens, I'll have him at the end of the day. And that's more important than anything else ever could be."

She's determined to make me ruin my makeup. I just know it. It's a small miracle that I manage to keep from crying as she presses her cheek to mine one more time.

"Now, it's time, wouldn't you say? I can't wait any longer to marry that man." She stands up straighter, smiles wider.

"Okay." I go to the top of the stairs and signal to Frank, who is waiting at the bottom. That's the cue for the violinist to move from the background music they are playing and into "Canon in D."

The guests, assembled in the drawing room, quiet down as Grandmother and I make our way down the stairs, hand in hand.

Frank opens the drawing room doors, and everybody turns in their chairs. The room's been emptied of all furniture, except the rented chairs, thirty in all. This is a much, much smaller event than Grandmother's first wedding.

But sweet and sentimental and meaningful just the same.

The room is practically overflowing with flowers, which is another of my grandmother's signatures. She might've wanted a small guest list, but by God, she'd have her flowers. Obviously, nobody was about to deny her.

As I make my way down the aisle, Hayley and Nicholas are wearing identical smiles. Grandmother insisted on inviting them, so there'd be young people for me to hang out with.

The next set of eyes I find are Matt's. Grandmother impressed on me that I did, in fact, need a plus-one. No matter how much I balked, she wouldn't hear of it. Matt gives me a discreet thumbs-up when I pass him, like he approves. And I very much approve of him in his tuxedo. Tall, dark, and handsome. The guy who's always there for me. My best guy friend. I'm so glad we made up and that he could be here with me even though he's dating What's Her Name. I give him a soft smile before turning my attention back to the front of the room.

Peter waits beside the judge, under an arch of lush pink and cream blooms. As if I wasn't already struggling to hold back the tears, he looks absolutely transformed. Radiant. Like a young man waiting for his sweetheart.

Our eyes meet, and I can't help but think back to that terrible night at the hospital, sitting at Grandmother's bedside. Witnessing his devotion, how completely dedicated he was—and still is—to her. Realizing he loved her, really and truly, and not as his employer.

And here we are.

I give him a wink before taking my place next to the judge. He smiles and then looks past me. Waiting for her.

The music changes, and the sounds of the "Wedding March" fill the room moments before everybody stands.

I can't stop the tears now. It's too much.

They only have eyes for each other, like the rest of us might as well not be here at all. I guess that's the way it is when two people have waited so long for this, when love developed slowly between them. Maybe neither of them even knew it at the time, the years when love took root and grew into something binding them together.

All these years, it's been the two of them. He was her most trusted and valued friend and confidant, the one person she could always turn to when she needed help or even somebody to sit next to while reading the paper. A companion.

And if nothing else, Peter is testimony to the fact that true, abiding love doesn't ask for anything in return. Because he never did. He just … loved her in little meaningful ways over the years. He never tried to force his love on her. It was enough, I guess, to make sure she was taken care of.

It's paid off.

"REMIND ME TO hire this caterer someday, if I ever get married." Hayley sneaks another hors d'oeuvre from a passing tray.

"If." I snort and roll my eyes heavily. "As if you won't. Please."

"Stop it."

"Stop what?"

She rolls her eyes back at me. "Stop putting ideas in my head. Nicholas and I are taking it one step at a time. We're not rushing into anything."

I wind my arm around hers and lean closer to her while we both watch Grandmother and Peter chat with friends. "Don't tell me you didn't get just a little misty-eyed, thinking about this being you someday."

She growls softly, and I know it's because she can't deny it. "That won't be for a long time. We're both way too busy and—"

"So, you've thought about it?"

"Of course." She says it loudly enough that a few people turn to see what the heck we're talking about.

I have to wait until the urge to laugh eases away. "Have you two talked about it at all?"

"No way. We're still trying to figure out what happens when his time here is up. That'll be coming soon, probably by Thanksgiving. Then, what will we do?"

"You take it one day at a time." I squeeze her arm. "Have you talked to anybody at the office about transferring?"

"I've planted the seed. Nicholas did the same thing with his office. I think the odds of my getting transferred are better than the other way around, honestly. He handles a lot of the West Coast clients. I sort of float around and help the senior associates as needed."

"I see." It's not easy to keep an upbeat tone, though I'm doing my best. "Well, I think you've already made up your mind. You're choosing the two of you, and that's the way it should be."

"But is it the right thing to do?"

I'm not used to hearing uncertainty in her voice. She's always so confident, sure of herself, with her feet solidly on the ground.

Which is why I give her a hug. "It's right if you feel like it is. In your gut. I trust you to make the right decision, always. I don't even trust myself half as much as I trust you."

She lets out a shaky laugh. "It's a big commitment."

"It is. You'll do great."

"Thank you." She hugs me this time. "You're the best friend in the world. Anybody else might try to sabotage things so I'd stay but not you."

"Maybe I want to get rid of you."

At least she's laughing when Nicholas finds us and pulls her away to where the drawing room has been transformed again. The chairs are scattered against the walls to leave room for people to dance if they want to. The music is quiet, sweet.

A soft sigh escapes me as I watch them together. She rests her head against his shoulder, and I swear, I can just about imagine her wearing a white gown.

"Hey. Why so sad?"

I look up at Matt, who somehow magically ended up next to me without me hearing him. "Just thinking about my best friend moving across the country."

"Come on. Let's dance."

He has my hand in his before I can say no. Not that I want to refuse him. No, this is just what I need right now. I need to be held even if I'm only being held by a friend.

"I'm happy for her. I really am."

His hand presses against my lower back, drawing me closer. "I know. Because you love her. You want her to be happy. That doesn't mean you have to be a total martyr about it. You're allowed to feel sad."

"Everything's changing. Even my grandmother is moving into a new phase of her life. And now, Hayley is too."

I glance up at him and find him already gazing down at me. "I mean, where does that leave me? I'm still in the same place I was before."

"You don't have to move at anybody else's pace. Things happen the way they're meant to happen."

I can't help but give him a skeptical look. "You believe that?"

"I do. What? You think I'm some kind of caveman who never has a deep thought?"

"No, I don't think that. All the time."

"Even now, I'm trying to be nice, and she has to make a snide remark."

"Sorry, sorry." I find myself leaning against him. He's extremely comforting. Familiar. And smooth on the dance floor. "You seem like the type of person who makes things happen. Who doesn't wait around for life to catch up to what he wants. That's all."

"Yeah, well, sometimes, life has a way of dragging its feet, and you have no choice but to wait. Even when the outcome seems obvious to you. You have to remind yourself that you aren't the only person in the world and that what you want isn't all that's involved," he says and something tells me we're not talking hypothetically anymore.

"Sometimes …" I have to take a deep breath and hope it slows the hammering of my heart. "Sometimes, life gets in its own way. Granted, sometimes, there are genuine questions and concerns."

"Sure," he agrees.

"And sometimes, it's easier to know a relationship won't last long by design. Because it can't, because you're writing books about the people you're dating, and ideally, there will always be another book."

"I can see that."

"Sometimes, a person just needs time to wake up. Open her eyes. Realize what's right in front of her." I sneak a look up at him. "You know, generally speaking."

"Of course. This is all general. Nothing specific. Any resemblance to actual persons, living or dead... well, you know." He shrugs. "You're the writer."

"I am."

The arm around my waist tightens. "What would you make of a guy who broke things off with a girl because she couldn't possibly live up to the girl he really cares about? How would you write that character?" he asks, his voice deep and sexy.

My heart is so full that I can hardly breathe. "Um, I think after putting him through his paces, I'd finally ease up and let him have what he wants."

We're not dancing anymore. We're not moving. We're staring into each other's eyes like there's nobody here but the two of us.

This is it. There's no going back now.

I'm in love with him. And I know he's in love with me. I feel it. I see it in his eyes, something I haven't seen in anyone but him.

"Everybody! Time to cut the cake!" Peter calls out.

Of course it is.

Suddenly, the rest of the room comes back into

focus. We're not alone anymore. We never were.

"I guess we'd better go watch them so Grandmother doesn't send out a search party." Though something tells me she wouldn't if she knew both Matt and I were missing in action.

"I guess we should." But he doesn't let go of my hand, and that's a good thing since I don't want him to.

I might not know how to move forward from this or what it means in the grand scheme of things, but right now, he's holding my hand.

And that's enough to make me feel incredibly happy.

ABOUT THE AUTHOR

Jillian Dodd is the *USA Today* best-selling author of more than thirty novels.

She writes fun romances with characters her readers fall in love with—from the boy next door in the *That Boy* trilogy to the daughter of a famous actress in *The Keatyn Chronicles* to a spy who might save the world in the *Spy Girl* series.

She adores writing big fat happily ever afters, wears a lot of pink, buys too many shoes, loves to travel, and is distracted by anything covered in glitter.